REVIEW

This final book in a moving trilogy begins when Harry's unnamed interlocutor tells his visitor "It's been a while. You seem changed since I last saw you." He recognizes "a change in the face, tension released, equanimity" in his visitor. We have followed Harry's long journey to this point, and now we hear what has transpired since the end of book two, "The Severed Cord." Harry and Jessica, grandchildren of WWI veterans, have recognized the source of intergenerational familial dysfunction – the cord that connected them to their grandfathers' mutual traumatic experiences during the war. Separately and together, Harry and Jessica are nearly capable of cutting that cord, of escaping "the ceaseless authority of past suffering". In a final journey they seek answers about the fate of Jimmy, Jessica's aboriginal grandfather and half-brother of Harry's grandfather. Their goal is to find the final link in the "the chain that had always dragged them low, into the mire of uncertainty and despair." They seek evidence of Jimmy's final years, after he abandoned his family.

The final journey transpires quickly, over a mere month. The first steps in the trek to follow Jimmy's path reintroduce Harry's skepticism about any kind of spirituality. This thread will reappear throughout the book, as Harry questions whether or not he can "park his skepticism and admit to the possibility of the divine". He's on the journey with a person who feels the answers they seek won't come from something that can't tie their thoughts and feelings together – won't come from logic and scientific reasoning. The action over the weeks engages and even endangers both Harry's and Jessica's families, with violence, illness, and serial manipulations that could stop less determined – and less newly confident – individuals from continuing. Harry persists, instead of running, instead of surrendering to his own "instinct for self-preservation." Through his growing capability for commitment, and his openness to the presence of "superior forces", he begins to become a positive influence within his own life and that of others.

Harry's newfound sense of equanimity as he relates the story of this journey has its original source in a new relationship with a woman who has already sought answers to the darkness in own her family's past. Rather than deny those negative influences, she has renounced their hold on her life. Anika has offered Harry a new path off the shifting sands of his past, a path that will allow him to face challenges and move forward. Her support of Harry's growth is confirmed when she tells him that she wants "to be part of it all", even as he journeys without her. He will need her strength before the story ends, as she joins the search. Unresolved relationships come back to life in unexpected ways, but the foundation he has built his relationship with Anika upon stands firm, and he begins to meet and resolve challenges, to accept accountability for his actions.

The beauty of this book is where it leaves us. Harry, Jessica, and Anika are together, and the journey to find Jimmy's resting place is finally concluded. All three experience a sort of spiritual sending that provides a sense of release. All of the new responsibilities and complications surrounding Harry are still there, but he now understands "his own part in the continuum." His shared journey and the support of both Jessica and Anika have given him" licence to submit to the present, to an abandonment of the self-destructive, to the acceptance of love."

There are so many deeply personal insights exposed in this book. Author Twartz makes the self-introspection meaningful and powerful, tying it deeply and effectively to the journey, to the action, and to each character. The first book in the series sent me on a journey of my own, and provided me with perspectives on my own behavior and its antecedents. I have to agree with Jessica. "What matters is understanding the past and how it's led us here. What matters is how we use what we've learned, how this can all mend the future." This book concludes with support for continuing our journey towards understanding, our search for reconciliation within ourselves and with others close to us. I am encouraged to continue my own journey.

— Rebecca Dodge, Emeritus and Adjunct Associate Professor, Midwestern State University

Author, Stephen Twartz's new book, *Woven Fragments,* is presented in masterful language, mystery and ghosts.

Harry and Jessica set out to walk in the footsteps of her Aboriginal grandfather, Jimmy. The roadmap of discovery makes them vulnerable to many experiences they encounter – "the spirits keep malign forces at bay." In the quest, Harry finds a cave of ancient art and contemporary drawings and stumbles on an old diary written by Jimmy – "a bible that defined a thousand generations." Jimmy's window to the past, exposes the misdemeanours of war and its consequences – "We can heal ourselves by understanding what those before us have been through."

There is great beauty seen on their journey – a "vast morning curtain draped about the horizon." These descriptions leave the reader with a sense of calm against the horrors and revelations of Jimmy's past, and the book becomes uplifting and one of hope for the future.

— **Judith Flitcroft, author of** *Walk Back in Time*

WOVEN FRAGMENTS

The sum of his actions

STEPHEN TWARTZ

Published in Australia by Sid Harta Publishers Pty Ltd,

ABN: 46 119 415 842

23 Stirling Crescent, Glen Waverley, Victoria 3150 Australia

Telephone: +61 3 9560 9920, Facsimile: +61 3 9545 1742

E-mail: author@sidharta.com.au

First published in Australia 2024   This edition published 2024

Copyright © Stephen Twartz 2024

Cover design, typesetting: WorkingType (www.workingtype.com.au)

ISBN: 978-1-922958-62-4

ABOUT THE AUTHOR

Steve is a sixth/seventh generation Australian, with Irish English/German heritage, a trained biologist, geologist, engineer and environmental manager working and living over many years across all states in Australia and four continents. He has been based in Western Australia for over twenty-five years and currently resides in Dunsborough, Western Australia.

Steve is driven to understand the lingering impact of trauma experienced by our forebears, the intergenerational influence of catastrophes such as war, flood and famine. The Veiled Thread Series: *The Veiled Thread* (2020) and *The Severed Cord* (2022) and now *Woven Fragments* acknowledge the genetic influence of the past seen by Steve as he lived and worked in various locations from Europe to North America, Asia and Australia.

Steve has maintained an active interest in the creative arts for many years as a writer and also as an artist, focused on Australia's south-west and the south of France where he lived for a time.

He lives with his partner Susie, dog Boodja and cats TC and Yala in Dunsborough, regularly surfing the large waves of Australia's southwest.

Other books by this author

The Veiled Thread

Severed Cord

Woven Fragments

Note: Each novel can be read separately and out of order.

To Susie who steadfastly supported me through dark days
and
To all First Nations people who still endure dark times

To Legacy, dedicated to caring for the families of those who served Australia, an organisation supported by veterans, servicemen and women, and volunteers providing support, care and guidance to the families of Australian Defence Force veterans who have given their lives or health.

*"The river rises, flows over its banks
and carries us all away, like mayflies
floating downstream: they stare at the sun,
then all at once there is nothing."*
The Epic of Gilgamesh

"Sometimes the heart sees what's invisible to the eye."
Alfred Lord Tennyson

*"Man is nothing else but what he purposes, he exists only in so far
as he realises himself, he is therefore nothing else but the sum of his
actions, nothing else but what his life is."*
Jean-Paul Sartre

TABLE OF CONTENTS

Chapter 1	Overtures			1
Chapter 2	Odyssey	August 17	*Morning*	7
		August 17	*Afternoon*	10
		August 18	*Morning*	12
Chapter 3	The High Country	August 19	*Morning*	17
Chapter 4	Change of Plans	August 20	*Night/early morning*	35
Chapter 5	Going Bush	August 24	*Morning*	45
Chapter 6	Plans Change Again	August 24	*Evening*	55
Chapter 7	Into the Wilderness	August 25		69
Chapter 8	Images	August 25		83
Chapter 9	Objective	August 27		97
		August 31	*Afternoon*	101
Chapter 10	Discovery	August 31	*Early evening*	109
Chapter 11	Perplexed	August 31	*Evening*	119
		August 31	*Late* evening	122
Chapter 12	Puzzled	September 1	*Early morning*	127
Chapter 13	Delving	September 1	*Midday*	133
Chapter 14	Diversions	September 3		145
		September 4		151

Chapter 15   Invitation   September 4   157

Chapter 16   Responsibilities   September 5   165

Chapter 17   Crisis   September 5   179

Chapter 18   Decisions   September 6   195

Chapter 19   Threats   September 9   209

Chapter 20   Confrontation   September 10   225

                                 September 11   230

Chapter 21   Endings   September 15   233

                                 September 20   *Midmorning*   235

Epilogue   245

Dramatis Personae   249

Chapter 1

Overtures

It seemed like an age since I laid eyes on the man, a lonely figure, trudging doggedly across the barren dunes that were built as steep walls against the encroachment of the sea.

Beyond the rolling surf, grey, foam-flecked, past the shifting sands that submitted to the will of storms, to the vagaries of the tempest, the spirits of our ancestors rode unceasingly with the beasts, great, slow bodies ignorant of the temporal construct. Fine wisps of vapour rose as they exhaled, warm flares that quickly dissolved in the cold air, fading like ghosts against the steely hue of the water, never reaching the flocks of wheeling, diving birds as they sought the fountainhead of life, the gathering, circling schools that would feed them all. Above, high above, the threads of cloud raced eastward, thin against the pale blue, fleeing, I thought, from the old day, from the storm that I knew would come.

The afternoon sunlight stretched across the ground as a bland vein, feeble, barely carrying enough energy to show the way, long shadows hiding the treachery of the biting waves, something I had watched over the years, the diminution of the land. The bay and the shore had always been a wellspring, to seaward the shallow sandbanks that protected the land, landward, the fertile plain stretching to a distant scarp, the remnant of misaligned continents, the cataclysmic parting of earth's crust. Now, the waves beat ever closer to the relic of time's passing, the sun forever fuelling change, some said irreversible; some days, weeks, the sun was absent, beyond the scudding, grey clouds, on others a baking orb, forever relentless it felt, as it dried and murdered the land.

Evening approached now, the shadows stretching into the dull of dusk, an icy breeze from the south making my eyes water, despite the heavy hood wrapped about my head, a sharp line of twisted clouds defining the transition, like some vast moving curtain draped about the horizon, endlessly growing, evolving, potent.

Before the billowing mantle, the clear evening sky fled from the day; an ethereal mix of colours that deepened as I watched, hinting at the starlight to come, budding perforation in the fabric of the universe, in the universal cloudscape of stars that enriched them all, that fell leaden into the tangled ocean, reflected in the folklore of my people.

Sheets of water surged along the steep beach, almost breaking over my feet, slicing vigorously at the crumbling shore, gnawing at the substrate, exposing shattered shelly fragments, charcoaled wood, clattering stones, remnants of some sunken lake, stream or field that once sustained them. Wisps of foam and spray drifted upward from the slap of the waves, carrying the pungent salt aroma to me, mixed with the faint eucalyptus tones of the land, the scrappy plants that clung tenaciously to life against the hostility of change,

change that had enveloped everyone, that forced adaptation against brutality, against the natural spite of the world.

I looked again to the man trudging across the sandy promontory, at the waves as they wrapped around the broken, disintegrating seawall, the last defence, I thought, before the mad rush of waves to the scarp. Still, that thought brought with it too much of the negative I had fought so hard to banish, the legacy I had determined would lead to places I need not go, to behaviours without value, without benefit, to me or anyone.

I heard the man's laboured breath now, carried on the wind, the kind of sound that signalled a long walk from the car park, implied physical stress, suggested too much of the easy life. The man's steps began to falter in the soft sand, loose deposits from the last storm, so many, so often now. A flock of terns swooped down to the wall as the man passed, jostling for position, faces pointing into the stiffening breeze. The man walked resolutely onward, a slight limp developing as he met the steep gradient of the water-washed beach.

The message borne on the wind, through the clear air, was simple: *my time has come, this visitor marks a turning point.* Throughout my time here, the decade of my isolation, I had managed to ignore the worst of the world, eschewing the meaningless chatter, the didactic, the dread, the terror promulgated by fashion, by trendy commentary. I had only ever received two visitors, the woman – girl, really – called Jessica, a seeker, I thought, seeking what, I wasn't sure, perhaps evidence of her past, proof that there was more to existence than the pointless consumerism that gripped humankind, the ephemeral whims of a culture in decay? What surprised me was how she had found me, returning every day for a week, questioning me, delving into my past, searching for references to old friends, associates, enemies. We ate breakfast, lunch, drank my peculiar variety of wine, sifted through my memory. Then she left, replaced, very briefly, by the man – likeable, but with an edge that revealed distress, grief he could not contain, loss that seemed to warp the fabric of his life.

I pinched my nose, shuffled my feet against the growing evening cold and nodded to the man making his way along the last stretch of saturated beach. 'Good afternoon, Harry,' I said.

The screech of the terns on the wall made Harry turn slightly, before answering, 'Good afternoon.' He paused as if listening to the plaintive cry of the birds. 'Long time no see. How have you been?'

'Doing well, thank you,' I said. 'In splendid isolation, no one to please, no one to disappoint. Perfect as always.'

'I've come a long way to see you again, to talk, about things we've found.'

I had always abjured the formal, the meaningless, redundant niceties that characterised so-called civilised society. I was convinced that such mutterings were merely a displacement activity, a verbal sizing of the opposition, a ritual to reveal gaps in defences.

Close now, I could see that time had treated Harry well; despite the heavy going across the sand and a slight limp, I saw a change in the face, tension released, equanimity that belied our last meeting. 'It's been a while. You seem changed since I last saw you,' I said.

I looked upward at the clouds, thin vapours now turning to

ballooning grey as the storm-front approached. *Change*, I thought, again, *the earth, the sea, the fretting of the land, humanity, this man.* I shook my head, wondering what circumstance could have drawn Harry here once again, could require a trek to this forgotten corner of the world.

'I've seen things,' Harry said. 'Things I can't explain.'

We stood mute for a moment, the stiffening wind buffeting against us.

'And you've come to me for an explanation?'

'Yes and no. So much I understand, so much I don't. I need someone who might help sort it out.'

'That's a long walk just for a conversation.'

'It's certainly been complicated getting to this point.'

I turned, walking towards the house, to the beckoning fire and the warm living room. As I crossed the short distance to the house, I said over my shoulder, 'Harry, come inside and tell me your story.'

CHAPTER 2

August 17
Morning

They left the beach house, with so much hope, Jessica to follow the trail of her grandfather, to discover the source of her generational loss, her fears, Harry to set a new path for himself, a restart after so many years of abandon, wasted affairs, lost self.

The drive westward from the coast, into the valley's depths, led to the steep, winding road, up a scarp to the broad basalt plain of the Monaro. The mountain's lush, almost tropical vegetation quickly surrendering to bleached grass on the treeless, rolling basalt plateau, the sky a clear faded blue that hurt the eyes after the low dripping cloud that crowded against the mountain range. Harry felt pangs of regret at leaving the beach house, its seclusion, memories of precious time, the spontaneity of each day, no plans, no demands, only whims and fancies taking them for long walks along the beach to the river mouth, north across the headland through tall forest to the lonely inlets and bays that he had explored as a youth.

'Nimmitabel,' Jessica said.

'Yeah, we'll be going through it soon.' Harry wanted to drive in silence.

'The place where the waters, the rivers divide,' she said. 'It's a word used by the people, the Ngarigo, who lived here before the whitefellas came.'

'Your mob?'

'No, my MOB comes from Redfern.' Jessica smiled as she emphasised the word mob. 'Not Jimmy's mob either; he was Kamilaroi or Gamilaraay from north and west of here, out on the western plains.'

'So, why are we heading up here, here in the mountains?'

Jessica drew in a deep breath, waved her hands before her, exasperation it seemed to Harry. 'Because, Harry, as I've said before, mum said rellies around Adaminaby had heard Jimmy was running cattle along the stock routes through the mountains.'

'When was this?'

'Just before and after the war, the second one.'

So much time passed, Harry thought, *how could they expect to find anything, any trace? He was a ghost, a vapour wafting away on time's breeze.*

'Jeez, lots of things have happened since then,' he said. "The Snowy Scheme for a start, earthworks, lots of valleys flooded, whole towns, including Adaminaby had to be relocated.'

'Yeah, but most of the old paths through the mountains are still intact. Pull your boots on. We'll be doing some walking.'

Harry fell into the reflective spaces of his mind. *Where would Jessica's relatives have gleaned knowledge of Jimmy's whereabouts,* Harry thought, *and why would a man who seemed to have wanted anonymity leave a trail for others to follow?*

'So, it's Adaminaby then,' he said, pulling himself away from pessimism.

'Yeah. The rellies have a nice place there, by the lake.'

'A good catch up with family?'

'Never met this mob before,' she said, 'but mum says they're nice.'

Jessica looked briefly apprehensive. 'They might be a bit leery of you, though, being a whitefella and all.'

Harry glanced sideways. 'And all?'

'Yeah, university educated, toffee-nosed, a right-wing, establishment, whitefella.'

'You've been to uni?'

'Yeah, but I'm a blackfella.' She paused. 'Part of the MOB, a blackfella!'

Harry quickly glanced at Jessica again, expecting to see a challenge. Instead, her eyes sparkled with humour, her mouth finally succumbing to a broad smile.

'Uncle Les is a teacher at the local school, and Auntie Gwen has a degree in geology and works as a hydrologist for the Snowy Scheme. I reckon they'll tolerate a corporate hack like you,' she said.

What could Harry say? He suspected the relatives already knew everything about him they needed to know.

*

August 17
Afternoon

Harry's introduction to Jessica's extended family had been brief. A night in Adaminaby, then the push into the high country. The house nestled in trees above the Eucumbene Lake, Jessica's relatives welcoming but guarded with a stranger – he had been warned. A veranda wrapped tightly about the house, the clatter of his boots on the boards reminiscent of a timber deck on a boat.

Harry leant against the balustrade, gazing absently into the distance, across the blue expanse of the lake, fingers of water forming inlets and bays fringed with a bare strip that delineated historical high water.

'The lake's not always been here,' said Les, thrusting a beer into Harry's hand. 'They built a dam across the Eucumbene River, fifty-six, fifty-seven. Had to move the town up the hill, away from the flooding.'

'Nice lake,' Harry said absently.

'Bloody cold, though, even in summer.' Les moved his vast bulk to the rail. The beam groaned at the assault; Harry pulled back slightly, wondering if the balustrade would collapse.

'I guess Jimmy wouldn't have seen all this,' Harry pointing at the distant lake.

'He could've, though we can't be sure.'

'Jessica says you've got evidence that says he came through here?'

'Yeah, well, I'm not sure its concrete evidence, but one of the old-timers here remembers someone called Jimmy, a blackfella.'

Les paused to take a slow swig from his beer. 'He was only a kid when they used to drove cattle through here. He said Jimmy was a veteran of the war and handled men like they were troops and horses like friends.

'Sounds like who we're looking for.' They both turned to words that came from behind.

'It's so long ago, Jessica,' Les said, turning to the voice. 'Back before the Snowy Scheme got going. The old fella remembers some things, forgets others, even has trouble recognising his own family at times.'

'Old folk seem to have trouble with the here and now, not the past,' Jessica said. 'When can we talk to him?' Jessica: no stone unturned.

'He's in an old folk's home in Cooma. Visiting only on Wednesdays and Saturdays.' Les paused, smiled. 'In the meantime,' he hesitated again, 'I can show you some of the spots around here, some of the historical spots. Might give you some background to the area?'

Jessica glanced sideways at Harry, slightly raising a questioning eyebrow. 'No pubs involved, are there, Les?'

'Might be, along the way. Travel is thirsty stuff.'

Harry couldn't see how travelling in an airconditioned car could increase thirst, but then, he would roll with the punches, no matter how many compulsory breaks.

'Tomorrow, then,' said Jessica. 'Early? On the road, say eight?'

Les nodded, Harry wondering what background they would see, doubting that wandering about the countryside would be helpful.

*

August 18
Morning

They stood on the parapet above the cascade, three of them, Les talking to Harry, Jessica looking the other way, down the narrow valley towards the vast flat plain, distant in the west.

Les pointed towards a brass plaque on a grey lump of stone that rose close to the concrete platform. 'They believed in the power of humanity,' he said. 'The power of mankind to change things, to control nature.'

Harry moved closer, the brass plate riveted securely to the stone, words dulled against the weathered metal, the last words glowing against the lowering sun:

... a testimony to man's dominion over nature.

'Can't see that man has dominion over anything, really,' said Harry, dusting off the words with his fingers, 'except maybe the third world unfortunates.'

Les raised an eyebrow. 'Yeah, well, different times then,' said Les. 'Back then, in the fifties, they reckoned anything could be controlled with concrete, technology, human ingenuity and brute force.'

'Pretty impressive, the Snowy.' Harry looked at the solid wall, the face of the power station.

A wry smile passed across Les' face. 'There'd just won a war. Thought they were invincible.'

'Probably were.'

'On the bones of the locals, the Walgal and Ngarigo people.'

Harry nodded his head. 'Yeah, Jessica told me about how the locals were basically destroyed by disease, the bugs brought in by the whitefellas.'

'And a fair sprinkling of treachery and brutality.'

'So, how do we track where Jimmy went if there's nothing left.'

'Not all of them were eliminated.' Could Harry detect bitterness in Les' voice? 'And there's plenty of campsites and sacred places in the mountains that haven't been destroyed. Gwen and I've done lots of walking through this country. Places we know, places I don't talk about to anyone.'

Harry shook his head. 'How will these places help get a fix on someone like Jimmy, someone who probably didn't want to be found? And anyway, it's a long time ago.'

'Dunno, Harry.' Jessica had re-joined the conversation. 'But we've got to try.'

'Good thing I brought some walking boots, then.' Harry always considered the practicalities.

Jessica smiled. 'It was me that told you to. You're an obedient boy.'

Harry took a deep breath, exhaled in a whistling breath. 'So, when do we start?' No use fighting it. Jessica clearly had planned for this outcome.

'First light tomorrow,' Les said. 'Start point just up the road from here.'

Harry pulled another draught of air into his lungs, looked along the road, then down the tight valley to the broad plain, below them, in the distance. It was rough country, precipitous. How would he cope with a steep climb? How would Les handle it, with all his bulk to manage? Jessica was lithe, light and barely noticed the rough terrain, but Les had found it difficult to manage his bulk up the steps to this slightly elevated place. Harry knew his own fitness was questionable as well - too much alcohol, too many long lunches and too many flights across too many oceans.

'How far to the sites?' said Harry.

'About ten-k's round trip.'

Doubts flared in Harry's mind.

'How long? I mean, how many hours walking is that?'

'About three hours each way. On the way back, most of its downhill, so a bit faster coming home.'

Jessica looked at Harry and laughed. 'Jesus, Harry. Are you scared of a little walk?'

Harry was silent for a moment, finally grimacing – deskbound for years, his time as a prospecting geologist a dim memory. 'Reckon I'll adjust,' he said.

'Well, you'll need to adjust quickly,' said Les, smiling. 'Gwennie sets a cracking pace. This is her country, and she loves a brisk walk.'

'So, you're not coming?'

Les cleared his throat. 'No way, too fat and slow, Harry. Too many beers, barbeques and classroom time. I'd just hold you up. Gwen knows all the places, and she'll be able to tell you lots about the country, the geology and the old trails running through the mountains.'

'Is that why we're headed into the mountains from here?' Harry said. 'There's stock routes through here?' Harry doubted there could be valuable trails for sheep, cattle and stockmen through these rugged hills and valleys.

'Yeah, not well known, these days or then. They used them to take cattle to and from the high pastures in summer.'

The unknown. Harry pictured the rocky path that led into the deep, forgotten parts of the mountains, the twists and turns of the trail, the air thinning as they climbed towards the peaks.

'So, gird your loins, Harry, tomorrow we head for the backcountry.' Jessica clearly revelled in Harry's discomfort.

CHAPTER 3

THE HIGH COUNTRY

August 19
Morning

One hundred steps don't sound like much, just one foot in front of the other, no weight to carry other than a small day pack and some water. Up the steep path from the car park at the road, breath coming in distressed wheezes, Harry swung his arms to maintain balance along the narrow, precarious trail, the ground falling away precipitously on each side. They climbed an exposed ridge that seemed to continue forever uphill. He dared not look upward, fearing his balance would desert him – a tumble, either way, leaving him somewhere down there, among the rocky detritus of the last landslide.

'How much further to the top?' said Harry, gasping for breath.

'Not far,' Gwen said, strong legs pumping, feet maintaining a firm grip on the loose shaly ground.

Harry fixed a stare at his feet.

'Come on, Harry!' Jessica gave him a gentle nudge from behind. 'We've just started.'

'I wouldn't do that, Jessica!' Harry waved a defensive hand

behind. 'Or you might be retrieving my broken bones from the ravine down there.'

'There's a rest stop a few minutes ahead.' Gwen glanced briefly behind her, smiled, accelerating her climb. Harry tried to keep pace, felt his thighs start to burn, his boots slipping against the rolling rocks.

'Not far.' Gwen shouted, now from a considerable distance ahead. Was that pity or concern he heard?

Harry took a chance, lifting his eyes, glancing ahead. Gwen's strong legs in shorts and boots disappeared over the brow of the slope. Where had she gone? He laboured on, legs starting to feel rubbery, sweat accumulating at his eyebrows, breath now expelling like steam from an engine. Harry wasn't sure how much more of this he could take, almost deciding to stop when Gwen's face appeared over the top of the climb.

'Come on. Almost there!' She disappeared again.

Harry trudged on. *Pump, you bastard*, he whispered between gasps, tapping his chest with a flailing hand, *pump*!

He didn't look up again until he felt the path gradient slacken, the path broadening, a slight easing of the pain in his legs, relief from a heaving chest. *This was a timely lesson*, he thought, *notice that life had become too easy. He needed this, perhaps not on the first day, but he needed exertion like this.*

'What was that all about,' he said. Gwen, leaning languidly against the face of an outcrop, raised a single eyebrow.

'I like to get the blood pumping first up, warm up. I find it sets you up for the rest of the day's walk.'

'Almost stopped me right here. I was ready to turn around, head down the hill, and in the car for a pint and a pie at the nearest pub.'

'You sound like Les.' Gwen looked serious.

It did sound like Les, Harry had to admit. 'But ...' He raised a hand, finger pointing to the heavens. 'I knew it would be good for me – character-building.'

Gwen smiled, her attention suddenly diverted over his shoulder at Jessica as she arrived at the rest point.

'What was that about!' Jessica said between breaths. 'You two took off like scalded rabbits.'

Harry turned to look intently at Jessica. 'Couldn't let Gwen get too far ahead.'

'Well, my legs feel like rubber after that climb. Too many roadhouse meals and too many hours slumped in the car.'

'That's the worst of it,' Gwen said as she turned to look up the trail. 'Easy going now.'

Harry followed her gaze, looking at the scattered path, at the loose boulders and tree roots fingering menacingly across the track. Harry couldn't see the improvement, except maybe the lack of extreme gradient. 'I guess it isn't like climbing Everest anymore,' he said.

'Come on. Have a drink if you need one, and let's get going,' said Gwen, laughing, 'otherwise, we'll be walking down in the dark.'

She turned and strode off along the winding, rocky track.

Harry looked at Jessica. 'She's gung-ho, isn't she?'

'She's a geologist, Harry. You should know they love bush bashing, or have you forgotten what they're like. Too many years gone by, have they?'

He could have taken umbrage at the remark, a biting remark surfacing, but he had to admit, had to agree, he was well past his days in the field, didn't want to return to them, had wished them goodbye with a significant degree of relief. He took a brief swig from his water bottle, drew a breath, smiling a Jessica. 'To rest is not to conquer,' he said as he turned, head lowered and marching after a rapidly receding Gwen.

*

'These places aren't well known,' Gwen said, walking across the snow gum-fringed space, sweeping the long, late summer grass aside with every step, 'for good reason.'

'Does there need to be any reason,' Harry said. 'It's pretty isolated here.'

Gwen had led them along a rugged path. They were on a rare piece of level ground, near to the edge of the escarpment, a light breeze rising from the west, the clear ground shielded from the worst of the wind by the gnarled, bent trees. There were few signs of any intrusion other than their own: the occasional bird flitting through the trees, the rustle of a lizard escaping from the path as they approached, dried wallaby scat from the previous evening's supper.

'Plenty. The spirits here keep malign forces at bay.'

Harry felt his scepticism rise – decided to say nothing, walking silently instead behind a purposeful Gwen. He could hear Jessica following him, rustling through the grass.

'I feel your doubt,' Gwen said, as she stopped, turning at a large, denuded granite outcrop.

'Doubt?'

'Spirits,' she said. 'Their existence.'

Harry thought for a moment. He considered his attitude: to the notion of spirits, their potential for reality, their impact on the world, on people, on himself.

'I was raised to deny belief in the spiritual.' He thought of his mother, her practicality, her repudiation of any sort of religion.

'I can feel it.' Jessica smiled as she looked about, to the grass, to the tops of the trees, to the heavens. 'Just let yourself go, Harry, submit to it.'

Harry didn't want to submit to anything, least of all to the ethereal. He remembered the wraithlike beings that had populated his childhood dreams, ogres driven from him by his mother's rigid shield.

'Spirituality,' he said. 'An overrated virtue. Faith in the emotive, the touchy-feely, the unprovable.'

'You're a cynic, Harry,' came from Jessica, in defence of her viewpoint.

'Not a cynic, a scientist.' Harry was supporting his training, his life, his belief in the power of rational thought and logic.

Jessica opened her mouth to speak, words stifled by her amazement. She shook her head, walking instead to the granite outcrop, her back to Harry.

'What?' Harry raised his arms, in defence or argument. Harry wasn't sure. He remembered then the Masada Fort in Israel, how he had gazed across the parched landscape towards the Sea of Galilee, and caught the fleeting glimpse of a horse that strode amongst the outcrop, wild and magnificent in its abandon. It had disappeared when he glanced away to seek corroboration from a bystander. Maybe, just maybe, he should park his scepticism and admit the possibility of the divine?

'The hut is through those trees,' said Gwen. 'No one uses it, no one knows it's there, except Les and me ...' she turned to point, 'and now you.'

'Who used it?' Harry squinted at the line of trees that bordered the far corner of the open ground, trying to penetrate the darkness that closed about the forest base. He couldn't see any man-made structures.

'It was used by the drovers that drove stock through the mountains. A stock route came this way.'

'It's well hidden.' Harry strained forward in the hope of a glimpse.

'That's probably why it's so well preserved. It hasn't been used since droving ended through here in the thirties.'

Gwen pushed herself away from the outcrop, turning on her heel, walking briskly to the clearing edge.

'Come on, Jessica,' she said. 'Let's take a look. See what you can find. Leave Mr Sceptic to his logical disbeliefs.'

The women strode into the forest, quickly disappearing into the shadows.

Harry stood alone for a moment, recalling the sensation, the way the fleeting vision of the Masada horse had taken him beyond himself, the discomfort of the inexplicable weighing on him for the remainder of his search in Israel for signs of his grandfather, of his time in Palestine so many years ago. He noticed the clarity of the air in this place, the lack of moisture, the brilliance of the light, like someone, something, had scrubbed everything clean, sparkling, almost translucent. Harry shook his head, feeling a slight ache behind the eyes, another reminder of the view from the Masada Fort, the harsh Palestinian landscape. The shadows of the forest suddenly looked inviting, hope rising in him that muted light would relieve the pain and provide some purpose to their search. He strode resolutely after Jessica.

*

The shade of the eucalypts descended about him, cool, the chill of the slight mountain breeze heightened under the low branches. Harry peered ahead through the tangle of foliage; couldn't see the women. They had disappeared so quickly. Where had they gone?

He swept his gaze left, then right, finally noticing a region of slightly flattened grass, tough grass that was springing back to hide the evidence of footfall. He would need to move quickly before the marks were lost, before he was lost.

A low branch made him duck. As he rose from a half-crouch, eyes looking forward into the shadows, he saw a figure in the distance, only a shadow. The figure seemed to merge with the bush, the image fading slightly as the sun was absorbed by a cloud. He moved cautiously toward it, hoping that it was one of the women. Then, a careless step, the snap of a twig, and the shadow dissolved, gone in the tangled mass of greenery.

Harry stopped: *probably a kangaroo or wallaby*, he thought, his imagination getting the better of him.

He moved forward, almost in a trance, stumbling over an exposed root. When he looked up from the near fall, he realised that the trail was lost; he was lost. His choice now: backtrack to the exposed granite dome or hunt around, hoping to find evidence of the women's passage. Time had elapsed since their feet passed through the forest; the grass would have recovered, markings on the ground gone – he didn't like his chances.

Harry stood, quietly surveying the surrounding forest, looking for guidance: which way? Forward or back. He could still find his way back. How far? A clue, anything to support a decision.

Movement ahead, the crack of a branch, the rustle of leaves. He remembered the saying: *guidance requires action.*

Decision made, he ploughed forward through the increasingly dense undergrowth – the last vestiges of a trail gone. But, then, he remembered the last part of the line: *but it does not guarantee safety.*

The foliage, branches, and undergrowth grew thick. Harry was struggling now to make headway, sharp twigs reaching out to probe at his face, to gouge into his eyes, the ground increasingly irregular, his boots sliding sideways into hidden potholes.

He remembered being in a similar state, many years ago, as a young geologist, fighting through a dense forest somewhere in Australia's north, separated from colleagues, unsure of the direction to deliverance. Finally, he had headed north as the only option; the river lay there, he would eventually stumble across its turbid waters.

A twig gouged his cheek.

He lashed out at the attack, lurching forward through a particularly dense wall of vegetation and …

Eyes half-closed, legs driving forward, boots drumming at the ground, the wall of foliage suddenly gave way to nothing.

Harry almost fell forward, arms flailing as he desperately fought to regain balance.

The narrow track was overgrown, clearly not used for some time. Harry looked left and right – no one in sight. The trail was definitely lost.

Where had they gone? Which way should I go?

Harry drew in a long breath, exhaled loudly, frustrated with the abandonment he now felt – *they could have waited*! Then, as he prepared a shout for attention, he detected a slight thinning of the forest to the left, along the abandoned track – a short walk to the clearing, and sunshine streamed through a break in the forest canopy.

'Harry,' said Jessica. 'Where have you been?' She immediately turned away, pointing to a dishevelled structure at the far edge of the clearing. The building was advanced in its decay; the ends of many of the wallboards collapsed to the ground. The timber roof was peppered with holes and the industry of walking and flying creatures. 'We found it,' she said, 'but there's not much left of it.'

'Not much left of me, either,' Harry said. 'I've been falling about the bush for ages, looking for you.'

'You could have kept up with us.' Jessica was unsympathetic.

Harry scanned the clearing. A broad, open area, obviously purposely cleared at some point, the stumps of old trees testimony to the industry of those who had built the shack.

Harry looked at Jessica, silent. The distant call of forest birds, the whistle of parrots, were the only sounds above the gentle whisper of the breeze.

'No one else here?' Harry said, as he turned to look about.

'Just us, Harry.'

Silence.

'Thought I saw someone, a man,' he said, doubt in his voice. The two women looked curiously at him.

'No worries, my imagination, a moment of disorientation, lost in the bush, probably a roo or something,' Harry said hurriedly, as he turned to the weathered structure – he wanted to put an end to this display of stupidity. 'Let's take a good look at the hut.' His eyes swept across Jessica's face as he turned. She looked carefully at him, her dark eyes seeking something, perhaps more of an explanation? The probe dug into his inner core, the secret places, his doubts, the things he denied. Was it something he had said that prompted this attention? His inventive mind, the glimpse of a figure in the bush? Or was it just his own reckless fixation, his careless obsession with women, craving the thrill of new affairs, the promise of renewal leveraged off another's vitality? He thought of Anika, wishing she had stayed, wanting her close. *I need a bulwark against myself,* he thought.

Harry shook his head, clearing away the dross, feeling tightness about his face, his teeth clenched as he walked through the hut portal, the sunlight suddenly dimming. *There's a strange feeling here*, he thought. *Not unfriendly, just odd.*

'I can feel something,' said Jessica from behind. 'A kind of clamminess.'

'Swamps, nearby.' Harry was in no mood now for the unusual – it had to be material.

'There aren't any.' Gwen's turn to inject some ghosts into the mix. 'I've walked all over the area.'

'Rain, then.'

'Not forecast.' Gwen was determined to bat away Harry's explanations.

Silence.

'Well, bloody imagination then,' he said, letting his frustration with wild fantasy show. 'What we've got here is a damn ruin, nothing more. I mean, look at it. Half the roof's gone, walls you can see through. It's a haven for spider poison and dead rodents.'

'Harry, it's more than that!' Jessica was quick to defend her belief in their search.

'How's that, Jessica?' Harry thought: *that's a bit harsh*, adding a softer, 'Are there ghosts here?'

No. That was still too harsh. 'Are we on the right track?'

Jessica drew a deep breath, turning to scan the broken dwelling. 'It's been untouched since Jimmy's time. It's on the trail he would have followed through the mountains and ...'

'And there's always been something secret about this place,' Gwen said.

'Yeah, stuck in the bush like this, no one would find it.' Harry clung to the material.

'No, I mean, secrets held close, like, it didn't want to be found.'

'Oh, come on, you two. There's nothing here! Just an empty wreck.'

Harry walked to a gap in the wall, grabbing at the loose boards. Even though he pulled lightly, one broke away, rotten, splintering as it hit the ground. 'See,' he said. 'It's dead. If he ever was here, any signs of Jimmy are long gone, decayed, buried, rotten like these walls.' Harry turned to the women.

There was a moment when Jessica was ready to mount a spirited defence. Harry could see it in the set of her legs, the tension in her face.

The three stood, a silent triangle, a silent impasse broken only by the growing moan of a heightening wind about the porous structure, the bending of forest branches, the high-pitched rustle of leaves, like the hiss of waves breaking against a sandy shore.

Jessica suddenly turned, breaking the standoff, marching out from the hut through the disintegrating portal. Harry followed, into the wide-open space, glancing as he went at the sky.

'I thought you said no rain forecast,' he said to Gwen, over his shoulder.

'None was,' she said.

'Those clouds look pretty black.' He pointed to a roiling, black mass that threatened rain. 'We need to get going. Reckon we're in for some bad weather.'

As Harry uttered the words, he felt the weather front arrive, a swift drop in temperature, the last of the sun's warmth consumed by gloom.

'Harry, we need to get something straight.' Harry looked up,

Jessica facing him, legs braced.

'What?' This was not the time for deep and meaningful discussions. 'We need to get going before the weather really closes in.'

'If we're going to come out of this with anything meaningful, we have to investigate every possible clue to Jimmy's fate.'

Harry felt frustration rise. 'Look, Jessica, we need to get going. The weather ...' He pointed skyward.

'And you need to open up to possibilities, things not necessarily in line with your damn scientific logic.'

Harry suddenly felt a strange detachment – as if he watched Jessica from above, her long, dark, curly hair tossed about by the growing breeze, a wind now, rising to a tempest that threatened to sweep them from the mountain; and several steps behind Jessica, the hut, dark, brooding, obdurate despite its fragility. Harry was impressed by the building's attachment to the ground, its stability against the heightening storm, its endurance against the grim tides of the earth.

'Harry.'

Harry was transfixed. He didn't want to lose this moment; it augured too many answers.

'Harry!'

Harry fought against the intrusion until the pain in his shoulder could not be ignored. As he looked to the side, he felt as if he was in a dizzying fall. Hands he recognised as strong working hands, those of Gwen, steadied his shoulders, softened his plummet to the ground.

'Are you alright?' The word came at him in a rush, the noise of the wind assailing his senses, rising to a shriek.

'We need to get out of here,' he said, striding to Jessica. 'Come on, we'll talk this through when we get down from this place.'

The journey back through the forest was straightforward, swift and direct. Harry thought: *Never one to take the easy path, am I.*

Spits of rain greeted the start of the trek across the flat, treeless plateau, gusting wind turning to a full gale as they approached the steep path down to the car park. Harry hadn't prepared for this; he expected fair weather, thin shirt, bare arms, face, all exposed to icy drops that now drilled deep into his flesh. Gwen hauled an oilskin from her small day pack.

'Expected dirty weather, did you?' Harry said against the roar of the wind.

'No,' Gwen said, shouting. 'This jacket lives in my pack.'

Harry looked at the narrow path, loose rocks slick with water, a snaking ribbon atop a spine that plunged over the lip of the plateau. 'I thought you said it would be easier going down?'

Gwen bent her head close to Harry. 'You can never fully predict weather in the mountains.'

'Well, this rain certainly appeared suddenly.' Harry began to wonder if other forces were working to blunt their search. 'I might be scooting down this hill on my bum before we're finished. The path is turning into a river!'

Gwen nodded, smiled, a nervous smile as she glanced forward at the path; her lips moved, she said something, the driving rain drowning the words. *No doubt, something encouraging,* thought

Harry. *Perhaps advising me not to slip, not to fall sideways into the abyss, not to end my days as a crumpled, broken mess in the ravine below? I would be mindful of such wise counsel.*

A moment to take stock before Harry plunged forward onto the slope, the gradient abruptly steepening, the loose shaly ground almost ending his ordered descent in the first few steps. He fought to stabilise, arms flailing, felt his heart lurch, the sweat instantly breaking out despite the freezing rain. *Survival? He would need to be more cautious*!

The path steepened, the rocks loose now, almost floating downhill with the growing torrent. Harry grabbed a quick glance forward, breath now coming in rasping draughts, tendons in ankles, thighs, hips stretched: the car park was no closer, lost in an icy mist that seemed to enfold them all.

At a slight lessening of the grade, Harry stopped, gasping for breath. He felt the warmth of a body behind him – he turned. *How interesting*, he thought, *that you could feel warmth with such cold*. Jessica stood close to him, hair, clothes clinging to her body, bedraggled, sodden.

'Keep going, Harry,' she said, barely audible above the deluge, pushing him lightly with blue-tipped fingers. 'This rain is getting heavier. We need to get to cover, somewhere warm!'

Harry turned back to the path and stepped over the lip, recognising as he moved, the place where they had rested that morning on the climb to the top. *Shit! The worst of the hill is yet to come, the really steep bit*, he thought. *But it's not far now.*

Later, he would recognise this as a moment of absolute stupidity, a moment of lost concentration, a moment that could have meant the end of everything, the end of their quest, of life itself.

His leading foot pressed down hard on the ground, the trailing leg swinging forward.

He was confident now that despite the vertiginous gradient, and the trail exposed to the buffeting gale, they would be there soon, in the car, on the way home to a warm shower, warm food, a glass of wine.

He felt his foot slide.

Shit!

His legs were in the air!

Fuck!

Like a slow-motion dream, he floated in the air, an age in flight before the bone-jarring jolt as he hit the ground, just below the base of his spine.

Shit!

The shale debris dug deep, gouging into flesh and bone, ripping a wide furrow into his lower back as he slid forward, down the slope. A shale pile preceded his fall, quickly building to a mountain, a bow-wave buoyed by the torrent of water. He gathered speed down the hill, swaying dangerously near the edges of the path, toward the near-vertical drop, to a doom he preferred not to test. His hands desperately grabbed at the ground on either side, the sharp edges of the shards slicing into his palms.

Orientation lost, Harry only had a sense of "down" and a primeval survival instinct – desperate corrections to his slide to prevent a plunge into the abyss – the pain dulled, vision narrowed to the immediate.

A heavy bump, a tumble – motionless!

Silence.

Harry heard the patter of rain, felt the splash of water on his face. Finally, he had reached a respite from his downward dive. Where was he – a broken body at the base of the ravine, pouring his lifeblood onto the rocks?

The sound of heavy breathing.

'Jesus, Harry, I know you were in a hurry to get down, but that was a bit extreme!'

'What?' For the moment, he could utter no other sound.

'Spectacular, if a little risky,' Jessica said.

Harry opened his eyes, Jessica's face hovering above him, concern in her eyes. The stream of water from the heavens forced his eyes shut. He breathed deeply, levering himself onto elbows.

'Anything broken?' Gwen had arrived.

Harry tested his arms, then legs, feeling returning to his extremities. 'Only my self-respect,' he said finally, sitting upright, examining the palms of his hands, blood welling from ugly abrasions, falling water smearing the blood to tiny, red rivulets. He slowly clambered to his feet, swayed slightly, limping cautiously across the road toward the carpark, to waiting warmth, a chance to recuperate and an explanation of what had happened – for that he would rely on Jessica, his inability in matters of the inexplicable, perhaps even supernatural, only too obvious.

CHAPTER 4

CHANGE OF PLANS

August 20
Night/early morning

The drive to the coast was quick; the traffic light, with only the occasional semi on the way from Canberra to the coast with supplies for hungry tourists as they crowded at weekends into the beach towns and resorts. They didn't stop in Cooma to interview the forgetful old-timer, despite Jessica's insistence: Harry was convinced of its futility and he had the steering-wheel.

Jessica sat in the front passenger's seat, huddled quietly into the depths of a down jacket.

'So, any ideas about what happened back there?'

Silence.

'I mean, like, why did Gwen take us up to that place.'

Silence.

'And, where did that weather come from?'

Jessica exhaled loudly; frustration, irritation or just a return to the real world? Harry wasn't sure.

'That bloody track almost killed me!' Harry glanced at the steering wheel, at his taped hands bandaged against the blood already seeping through the cloth.

Jessica slowly turned to look at Harry, drawing a deep breath. 'Harry, you're alive, the *bloody track* didn't kill you and ...' voice deliberately slow, emphasis on each word, '... we have to explore every possibility, no matter how slight or seemingly inane.'

'What did you expect to find?' Harry let his frustration surface.

Jessica was silent for a moment. 'I don't know.'

The wind noise about the car held Harry's attention for a moment, the black ribbon of the road undulating across the treeless, basalt plain of the Monaro. He opened his mouth, ready to insist on a return to some sort of realistic path, perhaps even abandonment of this fantasy.

'All I know, feel, I guess,' Jessica said, intensity, fervour, passion in her voice, 'is that he's out there, even maybe trying to contact us, somehow, somewhere. And I know if I don't try, give it every chance, take every opportunity, it will pass me by.' A pause; deep breath. 'And I'll miss what is critical to me and my family!'

Harry didn't know what *it* was; it was too ethereal, the notion too fragile for his blunt understanding of the universe. He understood rocks: the grinding processes that gouged and decomposed the solid earth, that spewed forth new continents from the bowels of the planet, that heaved and buckled the ground into mountains, valleys and ocean basins. The presence of wraiths, ghosts that imposed their will on the material world, fed his scepticism, reinforcing his cynicism, his dismissal of an alternative, a world beyond the purely mechanical.

And yet, Anika had passionately affirmed the profound influence of the past, not knowledge borne in historians' interpretation, but instead contained within the generations' secret thoughts, actions, and trials. Anika had found a sort of peace in her reconciliation with the past. Was this what Jessica sought? A reason for their predicament, explanations for the instability that ran through her family, that seemed to be preserved, nurtured, spread, no matter what they did?

'We're looking for the same thing,' Harry said. 'Only ...' He should just stop with that?

'Only, what?' Jessica was alert.

'Only ...' Harry hesitated. 'Only, you're always looking for ghosts, seeing them everywhere, when there's perfectly rational explanations for what you feel, how things appear.'

'You're telling me I've got an overactive imagination?'

'An imagination? Yes.' Harry smiled, trying to soften the criticism.

'But, Harry,' Jessica was caught in the gravity of her belief. 'Being scientific about all this, rational if you like, isn't going to get us far in our search. There isn't much scientific evidence to help tie our thoughts and feelings together.'

'Yeah, well, maybe we're on a hiding to nothing with all this?'

'Nothing or something?' she said. 'As I've said, I can feel we're on the right track, and we've gotta keep at it.'

There she goes again, Harry thought. *Led by her feelings, rational judgement cast aside.*

Harry's vision contracted as the broad, grass-covered plateau gave way to the forest. The Brown Mountain scarp was next, the lush fern-dominated foliage leading down into the valley, at the top the breath-taking view to the east and the distant coast, north to outliers of the Sydney Basin, south the ranges folding to the sea.

'Maybe, there's something practical I can do,' said Harry.

'You're driving,' she said. 'That's pretty practical at the moment.'

'No, I mean, something I can do to move the search forward. I reckon we're spinning our wheels right now.'

'What can you do other than what we're doing?' Jessica's turn now to be sceptical.

'Well, Jimmy drove cattle through the high country in the days before he disappeared. Is it possible he travelled to the coast, along those trails Gwen and Les talked about?'

'You mean the one from Thredbo down to the coast near Eden?'

'Yeah. The Bundian Way.'

'There's no one track, Harry, and some pretty rugged country.'

'But, the local people walked it every year, probably for thousands of years.'

Silence for a moment.

'Why would you want to do that, Harry? It's over three hundred kilometres from the mountains to the coast?'

A good question, Harry thought. He bit his bottom lip in contemplation.

'To use your lingo, we've gotta do something, and we've gotta keep at it.' Harry smiled. 'And after that bloody climb, I realised I needed the exercise and plenty of it.'

The car crested a rise, the last hill before the dip into the shadow of the mountain, into the dripping forest that clung to the scarp, the winding road cutting precariously through decomposed granites that had resisted ages of erosion, eventually feeding the streams and rivers in the valley below, crude gravels and rushing streams. Harry wondered at the obduracy of things, the desire, the need to continue, the evanescence and the tenacity of brutal fortune. He glanced up as the vehicle's nose dipped, and saw the sun-drenched valley far below, the gleaming ocean brushing against the coast in the distance. 'Yes,' he said. 'It's time I recovered some of my fitness. And who knows what I'll find along the way.'

Jessica – a wry smile. 'Ah,' she said, 'but will you make the distance?'

*

Sunday afternoon, the world turned suddenly cold, weather descending from the mountains to the west; with Harry submerged in the warm comfort of the beach house, the stove loaded with timber, the flicker and lap of mesmerising flames. Harry looked through the large windows, at trees bent low, a slate-grey sea tormented by a gale.

'You'll need supplies,' Jessica said.

'I think I need my head read,' said Harry, his shoulders suddenly shivering against the cold seeping through the glass. 'And wet-weather gear. Like Gwen in her secret oilskin.' He glanced at his hands, freed now from the bandages. Scabs were already forming about the wounds, the memory of his rapid ejection from the mountains.

'There's accommodation along the way, farm-stays and a few towns as well.'

She tapped vigorously at a keyboard. 'End of the first day, I can meet you at …' She paused, peering intently at the computer screen, '… at this forest lodge.'

He leant sideways on the couch to view the screen, laughing when he saw the image. 'They would call that rustic in the real estate agent's window.'

'As long as the roof doesn't leak. It'll be warm and dry, assuming you get that far.'

'Your confidence is encouraging.'

'It's rugged country, and the path won't always be clearly marked.'

'There'll be access tracks and fire trails for me to walk along if I get lost. And I'll have maps.' He managed an aura of confidence that he did not feel.

'Boots,' she said.

'Yes, I'll be wearing them.'

'No, you've got to pack spare laces. They're useless without laces.'

Harry took a deep breath. 'Listen, if I take everything I *might* need, I'll fall over backwards with the weight or end up digging holes with my feet with every step. Just wet-weather gear, a small tent, in case …'

'In case, what?'

'In case you don't turn up, in case I don't make it to our rendezvous, in case I meet some willing bird along the way and we decide to loiter in the wilderness.'

Jessica was silent for a moment, finally laughing – light-hearted scorn. 'Harry! Always the chancer.'

Casual infidelity – Harry realised it was now anathema to him. An image of Anika flooded his mind. Serene, quietly confident, her bold chin thrust forward, determined, eyes that penetrated, demolishing the wall he had built, probing his inner-self, subtly stripping away his resistance to intimacy.

'Talking about chances,' he said. 'I need to make a phone call before it's too late.'

He stood, urgency driving him swiftly to a private corner of the house. *Would Anika answer this time?* Messages were left, his hopes, his heart left hanging in the ether. A dial-tone, the dull click of the answering machine, silence.

Let her answer this time, this time, this time!

The phone rang, and rang, and rang – again the click of the answering machine. Harry rechecked the number. *Maybe she's changed phones*, he thought, not for the first time.

'Anika, Harry here. Hope you're okay. Been trying to get you. Guess you're busy. Ring when you can.' Should he say he loved her? Would it sound needy? Decision made, intimacy suppressed, he lowered the phone from his ear, and moved a finger to the "cancel" button.

A faint click stopped his finger.

Attention focused.

More clicks.

Disconnect.

Harry drew a deep breath, suppressed his disappointment, turning towards the door and the warmth of the lounge room. He would try again tomorrow. He subdued his growing disquiet. *Had she abandoned their relationship, found another lover?* His legs, knees weakened at the very thought.

A step towards the door.

The phone rang.

He snatched at the phone, stabbed at the "call accept", and slammed the phone to his ear.

'Harry!' An echo on the line.

'Anika!'

*

Harry held the phone tight to his ear. 'Anika, where are you? I've been leaving messages.' Instantly, he felt the selfishness of his need.

Silence for a moment except for repeated clicks.

Finally, Anika's voice broke through the silence. 'Harry, we've been in the Sundarbans. As you know, there's poor reception down here.'

Harry knew, but didn't care. 'So, you're still there?'

Anika's voice, distant now. 'We're headed for Khulna now, upriver.'

Harry strained to hear Anika's voice. 'What's that noise. I can't hear you clearly.'

More echoing clicks. Harry, irritated, shook the phone, an activity he acknowledged could only mean breaking the link. He desperately returned the phone to his ear – holding his breath, listening.

Clicks.

'... storm ... the wind ... cyclone coming ...' Anika's voice was disjointed, broken words stabbing at him.

'Anika, where are you now?'

Harry waited, not daring to breathe – he didn't want to miss any words that might seep through the tenuous connection.

'Harry, we're on the way to Khulna. The wind is ferocious here. The tide is swamping any dry land. The only chance is to head inland. Khulna is three hours away from ...'

Silence.

Harry pulled the phone from his ear and peered at the screen – call still connected, it said – hurriedly, almost throwing it back to the side of his head.

Silence.

'Anika! Anika!'

Silence.

Harry turned, flung open the door, strode back from the chill of the sequestered part of the house to the cosy warmth of the fire, the phone still glued to his ear. Jessica looked up towards the slam of the door. 'Harry, what's happened?'

'It's Anika,' he said. 'She's in trouble!'

'Trouble?' Jessica was standing now. 'What sort of trouble?'

'I mean, danger.' Harry drew a breath. He had to be calm. 'She's caught in a cyclone on the Bay of Bengal. Miles from nowhere. And the phone link died. The call failed.'

Harry remembered the isolation that was the Sundarbans, the intricate pattern of tidal channels, muddy islands, crocodile-infested mangrove swamps that constituted the northern Bay of Bengal coastline – so many watery pathways, all exposed to the fury of storms, to the tempests that descended onto the hapless and helpless of Bangladesh.

'Why is she there?' he said, unable to hide his frustration. 'She should have been in the north, away from the coast. They give days, at least a week's warning before these storms make landfall.'

Jessica shook her head. 'Who knows, Harry. From what you've told me about Anika, she cares about people. Maybe she's trying to help.'

'Like King Cnut, you mean, trying to hold back the tide, convinced of her own divinity? he said.

Jessica's eyes narrowed, a peeved set to her mouth. 'Harry, that's unfair!'

Harry immediately regretted his cynicism. Anika knew well her limitations, was devoid of narcissism, carried a genuine concern for others. 'Yes. That was unfair. I'm just worried, scared shitless, actually. And there's nothing I can do from here!'

'You mean, you can't do the Jesus thing, turn water into wine, walk on water, cure the sick and the lame, turn back cyclones?'

Harry held Jessica's eyes for a moment. 'Yeah. I get your point.' He sprawled heavily onto the lounge, once again keying in Anika's phone number, the chime of the dial ringing clearly through the room. The call sequence reached its end, a brief silence, then a "call-failed" signal. Harry felt the crush of negativity, of pessimism that he had fought so hard to banish. Maybe he was destined to live with the burden of nihilism? He shook his head with denial, repudiation of fate. The choice was his!

'I'll keep trying,' he said. 'There's bound to be comms in Khulna.' Harry breathed in deeply, bit his bottom lip, exiling dark thoughts. 'In the meantime, let's get back to this walk to the coast.'

Jessica resumed her seat on the lounge next to Harry, pointing to the laptop screen, 'You need maps,' she said. 'We can buy them here.'

CHAPTER 5

August 24
Morning

Harry parked beneath the tall eucalypts in the small bush lot, several kilometres to the east of the river, a meagre stream that flowed sporadically in response to occasional good snow seasons in the high mountains to the west. Jessica chose this as the beginning of Harry's trek because the rudimentary maps suggested the trail to the coast passed close by; and belatedly mentioned that several of her relatives happened to live in the nearby town.

Harry was bending low beside the car, fiddling with his small backpack on the ground, Jessica leaning over a map spread across the bonnet of the vehicle when a vehicle approached along the rough dirt road and stopped beside them, a cloud of dust billowing about the car's battered carcass.

The driver flung open the door, got out, hinges protesting; a man, unshaven, beanie pushed low. He stood assessing Harry and Jessica, one hand gripping the top of the vehicle. Finally, he moved from his silent observations, walking around the back of the car, between the cars, across to Jessica.

'Where you been, sis?' the man said. 'We was expect'n ya this morn'n, at home.'

Jessica turned to face the voice. 'Planning a walk.'

The man nodded. 'Weather's likely to turn nasty this afternoon. So, don't go too far.'

'Not me,' said Jessica pointing to Harry as he straightened from examination of his pack. 'Him.'

The man turned to face Harry, smiled, a knowing grin, offering his hand. 'G'day, name's Jim.'

Harry glanced at Jessica. 'Yeah,' she said. 'After our grandfather.'

'Nice to meet you, Jim. How did you find us?' asked Harry with a firm grip, a vigorous shake of the hand.

Jim laughed. 'Not hard. Almost the whole town saw y'arrive.' A pause, patting his jacket pocket, dragging out a packet of cigarettes.

Harry stepped back to get a better view of the man. 'No secrets here, then.'

Jim struck a match, lighting a spindly roll-your-own, shielding the flame from the light breeze rustling through the eucalypts at the perimeter of the clearing. Tall, straight back, Harry had to bend his neck to look at the heights, fighting back the impulse to ask: *what's the weather like up there.* The weather-beaten face was deadpan, but he could imagine emotion could take it to extreme places, that violence wasn't far away, controlled now by family. He resisted the urge to edge closer to Jessica.

'Well ...' said Jim. Harry sensed reticence. 'Not amongst us locals. Most are family, like.'

'Closed shop?'

'Not exactly. There's fellas from north of here that do business with the locals. We trust *them*.' A pause, a shrug of the shoulders. 'Well, sort of. At least when we can see'm.' A laugh.

Humour changed Jim's face enough to raise doubt in Harry: *had he misjudged the man?*

'It's the coppers we really don't trust,' Jim said with a vehemence that confirmed the judgement, the verdict, the sentence.

'What? The bent ones?' Harry immediately regretted the comment, suddenly feeling that he was asking too many questions.

Jim looked at Harry for a moment, mouth tightening, as if debating the wisdom of continuing such a conversation. It seemed to Harry that there was a withdrawal, a reversal of the initial openness – Jim jammed his hands purposefully into his trouser pockets, looking down at his feet, shoulders slightly hunched.

Silence, except the rustle of the wind in the trees and the chatter of birds in the valley below.

'No,' Jessica said, stepping between the men, the map left flapping in the breeze. 'It's the honest ones, the ones that can't be bought. Isn't that right, Jim? The ones that get in the way of your business.'

Jim grunted, a reluctant sound, throaty and perhaps resentful. Harry wondered whether it was an affirmation of Jessica's comment or a repudiation – then decided it didn't matter. What mattered was whether *the business* would affect their search, present any obstacles, any diversions.

Jim stirred from his retreat as quickly he had entered, straightened to full height, and smiled. 'Too right, Jes. Too right.'

And that seemed to be an end to the lingering tension. 'Now, which direction are you headed, Harry?'

Harry suddenly realised he had been holding his breath; he exhaled, reloaded with a deep, fresh draft of air. 'Towards the coast. Into the Bondi Forest, I guess.'

'All the way?'

'What do you mean?' Harry shook his head, attempting to release himself from the previously tense mood.

'To the coast?'

'Oh, yes,' he said, focusing now on the conversation. 'All the way. If the trail goes that far.'

'It's at least four days to the coast from 'ere, walk'n ten hours a day.'

'And I'm looking for signs of use, those who used the trail over the years.'

Jim thought for a moment. 'We use bits of it, not all of it, but I've never seen any signs other than recent stuff left by them fellas from forestry and the Land Council.'

'No huts, no old campsites?'

'Used to be.' Jim leant forward, across the vehicle bonnet, flattening the windblown map with his hand and forearm, waving a finger at the vast area of green. 'But the forestry mob have cleared away most of it.'

Harry sank under the news: *what use was this effort? Too many years passed, too much had changed.*

'It's like in the high country with Gwen,' Harry said, turning to Jessica. 'Nothing's left.'

Jessica ignored Harry's pessimism. 'A lot of it hasn't been touched by Forestry, not walked through for years, protected as critical water catchment.' A pause to draw breath. 'There'll be signs of who's used this trail, even now.'

The desperate optimism was obvious – was this false hope, delusion in the face of rapidly narrowing options, Jessica's last hope? Harry stood quietly for a moment, sifting through the images, the misgivings within him that dogged everything – suspicion, scepticism, doubt. He drew another deep breath, searching for the feeling of the earth beneath his feet, looking for resolve that he knew was thin in the face of such feeble evidence.

'Well,' he said, reaching for the map, looking at the sky, at the angle of the mid-morning sun. 'If I don't get going soon, I won't reach the Bombala road by nightfall, Jessica won't find me, and I'll be stuck in the middle of nowhere for the night.'

Harry hoisted the small pack, swinging it onto his back. He stamped feeling into his feet, sensing the tightness of the boots, arches irritable in anticipation of the trek. He tramped across the open ground to the gap in the foliage, the opening to the trail into the wilderness, to the unknown, wondering what *business* Jim had in the Bondi Forest, business that attracted the unwelcome interest of *honest* coppers. Jessica seemed to know but was clearly unwilling to elucidate – knowledge strictly confined to family, it appeared, forbidden to strangers like himself?

He brushed aside the undergrowth, grasping foliage that imposed itself about the entrance to the trail, plunging onto the steep, rugged path, down to the promise of enlightenment in the valley beyond. *A good walk*, he thought; *that's what I need to give me time to think without the incessant chatter of others as a distraction.*

He felt the probing leaves and branches brush his back, an end or beginning he couldn't tell. Did it matter? Life was a series of *endings* and *beginnings* that so often passed unnoticed. Maybe, just maybe, this was a portal to a new start, the image of Anika once again filling him, brushing like the errant branches across his mind.

*

Harry stepped across the stream, the water flowing over his boots – the rocks were slippery, the hour late, his feet tired, he had missed the stone. Now, his socks were wet! He looked up into the tree canopy, at the slightly misty air, the rays of the sun fingering through the leaves, stretching towards the ground. *God's fingers*, his mother always said, *out of the clouds, feeling, searching for hapless creatures on the land*. His mother always tried to put the fear of God into him, often succeeding.

He stood for a moment, in thrall to such splendour. Maybe there *was* a divine being, a supreme commander moving the pieces on life's board. He shook his head, wondering whether even such a short time in the bush was addling his brain, brief isolation leading to permanent insanity. Still, the beauty held him, binding him to a dimension he had not felt in years, not since those early days working in the northern bush, remote, ancient, sacred, the tiers of history ramping above the land, scored cliffs standing testimony to the survival of generations. He closed his eyes, feeling the slight movement of the air, sensing the deep, pungent aroma of the leaf litter, the acrid emanations of the eucalypts, drawing in a deep breath.

He opened his eyes, shaking his head. Maybe he was letting the moment get away with him, emotion ruling reason, the reign of imagination over the indisputable. He listened to the sounds of the forest – quiet now, a lull in the afternoon sun, even the birds suddenly quiet.

A crack! The sharp sound echoed through the forest.

Harry glanced about the dense undergrowth that crowded the stream – tense.

Nothing.

No movement.

The faint afternoon breeze had backed to a soft whisper. Was it just a falling limb, a branch fatigued by ages of alpine winds, shaken loose, finally submitting to gravity's call?

No further noise.

Harry relaxed his shoulders. *What was he thinking – that there was some kind of looming threat?* He had walked all day without seeing man or beast, except for birds high in the forest canopy. This was a benign country, untrammelled by the wilderness fanatics that frequented the trails about the high mountains to the west.

He stepped clear of the stream, the squelch in the boot making him bend to pull at the top of the sock. He stumbled slightly as he climbed the creek bank, his hands pressing flat against the ground, lucky not to plant his face into the moist soil. How much further did he have to walk before meeting the road? Would his wet feet hold out?

He steadied himself at the top of the bank, still crouching low amongst the foliage, when ...

Another sound – this time insistent.

Harry froze!

Voices!

What made him fear exposure?

He carefully parted the branches and leaves. Nothing – he could see nothing this close to the ground.

Anger!

Another crack! This time he recognised the sound – not a falling limb.

Silence.

Harry slowly raised his head, just above the tops of the bracken. Two men in a clearing: a man standing over a prone figure, a small object in the standing man's hand, no movement on the ground. The upright man raised his hand, pointing the thing at the ground.

The crack of a gun echoed about the forest.

Harry ducked, hugged the ground, tasted the earth, the loamy greasiness, praying that the wheeze of his breath would not give him away.

The wind in the trees, building now, penetrated deep into the undergrowth, velvet-soft wisps brushing against Harry's cheeks. He dared not move, tried not to breathe, felt cold, and moisture seep upwards from the ground, into his chest, into his head, into his heart, cold that seemed like it would freeze, taking from him any chance of flight, any possibility, should he be discovered, of survival. He lay still, an eternity it seemed, hearing straining for the slightest notion of movement in the clearing beyond.

Nothing. Just the pulsing rush of wind now gusting amongst the tree-tops.

Half an hour, maybe more? He wasn't sure, but the light was fading with a lowering sun. Time to move? Would they be waiting, patiently mocking his hope for escape, flirting with his pitiful prospects?

Harry took a gamble. He backed down the bank, scrabbling desperately with his boots, hoping the uncontrolled drop to the creek bed wouldn't dislodge stones in the loose, crumbling slope. He glanced desperately along the stream as his boots landed roughly on the slippery rocks. Which way? Which way to safety, to freedom? What if they were waiting along the trail?

He stood – indecision. Then he fled, along the creek, water pouring into his boots, fear, terror driving him to the east, where he hoped Jessica waited on the road, the forest track that led to safety and warmth.

.

CHAPTER 6

PLANS CHANGE AGAIN

August 24
Evening

'One of those snub-nosed things,' said Harry as he lingered in the warmth of the vehicle, the blast of air from the vent roasting warm against his face. 'Like a shortened rifle or shotgun. Hell of a racket when it went off.'

Jessica eyed Harry, doubtful, probing. 'Who? Who was it?'

Harry was silent for a moment. 'Not sure,' he said at last. 'They were at least a hundred metres away, at the edge of the clearing, in the shadows.'

'Someone was injured, you said.'

'I'm not sure, Jessica.'

'Why not? You said you had a clear view.'

'Like I said, they were a fair way away. And I didn't stick around to find out.'

'They didn't see you?'

'I backed up to the creek, crept along it for a while, kept my head down and then just ran.' Harry felt a pang at his abandonment of the scene.

'No one followed?'

'No one seemed to be behind me.' Harry wasn't sure. He didn't want to admit that he'd been too bloody scared to check properly, that maybe he recognised the shooter, that there was shouting, screaming, as he hightailed it out of there.

The getaway had been treacherous, stumbling over rocky ground, over the uneven river stones, his feet tired, rubbing raw against slippery wet socks, and he was sweating profusely, moisture soaking through his shirt, rivulets running down his back.

He stopped, the sound of his heavy, faltering breath drumming in his head. Was that screaming? Distant now, staccato, fading. He looked up. A flock of birds, white cockatoos, screeched through the canopy.

No! His imagination!

He slumped against a large boulder, the clear creek water sluicing about his feet. He shifted his backpack to take the weight from his shoulders, drew a deep, shuddering breath, the cool air gradually seeping through his body heat.

Imagination.

He wasn't noted for his imagination, a propensity to hysteria, susceptibility to panic. Yet ...

Was it imagination that had prompted such panic? Had he run in the face of raw violence, anger that appeared to take a life, or was there another explanation for what he had seen? Or thought he saw?

Harry suddenly noticed the cold, its tendrils penetrating his body. How long had he been sitting here? He looked skyward again – the sun now throwing long shadows about the forest.

He stood, the ache of his muscles a testimony to the slow penetration of cold mountain air, his idleness, and, he hated to admit, to resilience-sapping age. He looked upstream, listening desperately for evidence of pursuit.

Nothing.

No time to waste, he thought. *Jessica will be waiting at the fire trail.* He needed to move quickly now if he was to reach her before dark. He turned, searching for the track that followed the creek to the rendezvous, somewhere to his right.

Harry took a deep breath, turning to look at Jessica, the blast from the car's heater forcing an involuntary shiver. The evening was quickly lowering, her delicate features, brown skin, dark, liquid eyes softly illuminated by the car's instrument lights. The shock of the events in the forest still endured as a dry, nasty taste in the mouth. 'Look, let's just get to the accommodation. We can decide what to do from there.'

Jessica continued to quietly observe Harry, mouth opening as if about to talk.

'Look! Jessica!' Harry jerked his hands, synchronising with his words, frustrated. 'I'm not imagining any of this. I'm not a hyper-imaginative schoolboy. There was a gun and a body on the ground. I just didn't stick around to ask the way, get the details.' Harry knew he was obfuscating, delaying the inevitable question.

'Maybe we should go back and find out,' Jessica said, finally finding a chance to voice her thoughts.

'Go back!' Harry was shouting now. 'What for?'

'They'll be evidence.'

'What! The body left there?'

'Maybe.'

'Look, Jessica, guaranteed the body will be gone. It's probably six feet under by now.'

'Well then, the grave!' Jessica huffed an exasperated huff that shook her head, swelled her cheeks, and squinted her eyes. 'Maybe blood on the ground, some cartridges from the gun?'

'Let's just sleep on it.' Harry tried again. He didn't want to return to that place, didn't want to delve into the details of what he saw, or scrabble around for evidence of a crime.

'Shit, Harry. Are you a man or a mouse?'

Harry didn't need to think. 'A duck,' he said. 'And this little black duck wants time to think it through. That shooter might still be hanging around.'

Jessica huffed again, and turned to face the front of the car, grasping the steering wheel.

Silence except for the noise of the air rushing from the vent.

'Bloody hell, Harry!' Knuckles white, clenching the wheel. 'I leave you alone for a day, and you turn up this mess!'

What could he say to that? Not his fault? He didn't ask to be a witness to an assassination? Let's just forget about it and move on? We've got more important things to pursue, like walking all the way to the coast? He felt the weakness of his desire to escape.

'We need to talk to the police,' Jessica said through gritted teeth. 'At the very least.'

'No!' Harry felt a flash of panic.

'Why not?'

'You heard what your brother said.' Harry fought to keep his voice steady. 'They're likely to be in on it.'

'What?' Jessica's face, her voice, saturated with disbelief.

'And you agreed with him!'

'Are you suggesting that Jim is involved in this somehow?' Harry felt the encroachment of the truth.

'I don't know, you don't know,' Harry said, again trying to divert from the inevitable. 'But what I do know is something's going down in that forest, and it's not nice.'

'Bloody hell, Harry!' Jessica could not be diverted. 'Was it Jim you saw in that clearing?'

'Jes,' Harry desperate now. 'Like I said, I can't be sure.'

Jessica could not be fobbed-off. 'On the ground, or with the gun?'

It felt to Harry like a tide rushing over his prone body, a deluge shifting his body about, abandonment of any control over his fate. He had to delay his response, calm the mood, recover an equilibrium. He could see no way.

'On the ground,' he said finally.

'Shit!' Jessica shifted from concern to panic. She grabbed for the door handle, readying for a leap into the growing dark.

A whack on her driver's side window – solid, rapid, urgent.

Jessica screamed, Harry started, a face appeared at the window, blood streaming from its scalp, mouth set in a grimace.

Harry flung open his passenger side door, clambering around the front of the vehicle, to the man, a dishevelled figure standing, stooping in the light of the car.

'Sure glad I caught you here,' said the man.

Harry, silent for a moment, finally said, 'I thought you were dead.'

'No, can you believe it, the bastard missed me, from point-blank range as well.'

'Jim!' Jessica, now free of the car, arms wrapping tightly about her brother.

Harry took a step backwards, observing the reunion, unsure where this left their search. *Maybe*, he thought, *Jim's antics would stifle Jessica's enthusiasm for the venture, and he could go home? Wherever that was.*

A cold gust of wind cut through the growing dark, slicing into his chest. Well, at least to a warm, comfortable night.

'Enough!' said Harry, returning to the protection of the car. 'Let's get somewhere warm.'

*

'I kicked him in the balls,' said Jim, Jessica carefully dabbing at the laceration on his forehead, dissolving the crusted blood. 'He went one way, screaming like a bloody girl, and the bloody rifle went the other.'

Harry shook his head. 'You're bloody lucky. Another millimetre and the bullet would have gone through your skull.'

'No.' Jim laughed. 'He let go of the damn thing, the butt whacked me in the head, then went off when it hit the ground. That prick was rolling round, holding onto his family jewels. Didn't know where his gun was.'

Harry looked at the dishevelled man: the jagged forehead

wound, bruised left eye, lacerated arms, torn shirt, wondering whether the whole truth had been revealed, whether he should probe further into *family* secrets, Jim's business.

'So, why the fight,' said Harry. 'And where's this fella now?'

Silence descended on the cabin, Jim tensed, Jessica glancing up at Harry as she continued her repairs, a warning glint in her eye, but Harry had to know.

The silence extended to a long, awkward quiet. Harry readied himself to continue his questioning when Jim raised his eyes, his hand softly pushing Jessica's hand from her ministrations, then stood, turning towards the cabin door. *He's leaving*, Harry thought. *I've crossed the line, and now he's pissed off by my prying.*

But, Harry had to know! Damn the consequences.

Jim walked to and opened the door, a blast of frigid air eddying through the warm room. Harry could see the lash of the trees before the hut as the wind, the cold air drainage from the high mountains, gathered its nocturnal pace. Were the gods demonstrating their displeasure, their wrath, their anguish at the deeds of man?

Jim stopped, grasped at the door frame, leant through the door, looking left and right outside the hut. Apparently satisfied with the result, he stepped back into the room, firmly closing, latching the door, and turning to Harry and Jessica.

'You know where the owner of this place is?' Jim said.

'No.' An exasperated edge to Jessica's voice. 'No one was here when I arrived. They left a key in a lock-box.'

Jim stood by the closed door for a moment, silent, holding his focus on Jessica, searching her face, deadpan, eyes occasionally flicking to Harry. They were being assessed – were they trustworthy, reliable? Harry suddenly wasn't sure he wanted Jim to confide in them, whether their knowing the cause of the fracas in the forest would benefit anyone. Seized by sudden foreboding, Harry moved forward, ready to deny his need for information.

'Drugs,' Jim said as if that revelation explained everything.

'What?' Jessica's response was loud, almost a scream.

Jim moved forward, sitting heavily on the dilapidated settee, an air of resignation.

'What do you mean, drugs?' Jessica's anger growing.

'In the forest.'

'The forest? Where?' Jessica, chin thrust forward, belligerent. Harry took a step backwards – he didn't want to be ensnared in this tête-à-tête; there was no point in being exposed to an artillery barrage. Jessica meant war; he could be seriously injured. How could someone so small, delicate, petite, transmute so swiftly into such a fearsome being?

'Near the stream where I got this.' Jim tapped his bloody forehead.

'What sort?'

'What'd y'mean?' Was Jim dumb, or did he have a death wish?

'The drugs, what sort?' Jessica's voice was now even more menacing. Harry backed away several more steps, wanting to leave, fearing any focus of attention on himself.

Jim shuffled forward on the seat, bracing himself to stand, to no doubt escape to the relative peace of the forest beyond the dwelling.

'Sit!'

Jim, the dog, and Harry obeyed.

'What sort?'

Jim took a deep breath, remained silent, his vast bulk shrunken now, cowed on the bench, submissive in the face of Jessica's tirade.

Harry watched, mute, as energy built in the air between the siblings, sensing the gathering of a violent, jagged electrical discharge. He had to say something, something to prick the growing impasse, anything to drive the conversation to a conclusion, an admission that would give an explanation to the day's violence.

'A customer, Jim?' Harry's voice stabbed through the silence, his head in the lion's jaws. 'That bloke you were fighting with?'

Jim glanced at Harry. Was that relief in his face, or were there lines of worry, of guilt?

'Yeah.'

'So why the fight?' It was time to persevere.

Harry saw the lines, saw the worry. 'The bastards decided not to pay us.'

'Us?'

'It's a family business, not just me.'

Harry glanced at Jessica – her mouth a tight line. She shook her head. 'I'm not part of this, Jim. All this is news to me.'

'Pay you for what, exactly?' Patience, persistence – Harry now wanted the whole story to come out.

'The gear we were growing, the grass.'

'Right.' Harry had one link in the confession, now for the rest. 'And who was the dude with the gun?'

'A bastard from Sydney.'

Harry was silent for a moment, thinking through the scant data. 'So … let me get this right. This bastard from Sydney didn't want to pay you for your latest crop,' he said, at last, a summary like a peg in the sand. 'And …'

'Yeah.'

'Come on, Jim! And this bastard attacked you with a gun? For a measly bunch of grass, he was going to murder you?'

'Well, yeah.'

Harry's turn to shake his head. 'What was he, some sort of psychopath, deranged, something out of Mad Max?'

'No. A bastard from Sydney.' Jim's unease had returned.

'Yeah, heard that description before.' Harry half-turned away, glancing again at a silent Jessica, abruptly turning back to a browbeaten Jim. 'There's something you're not telling us, Jim. Who was that guy? Why did he want to kill you?'

Silence.

An audible, deep breath from Jim. Harry could see emotions playing about Jim's face, frustration, distress in Jessica, the strengthening wind hammering at the cabin roof and walls. 'Who was he?' Harry pressed home the interrogation.

'A copper,' Jim said at last.

Shit!

'Came down look'n for me because I took their money, but didn't deliver the goods.'

'Didn't deliver? Why?' Jessica entered the grilling.

'Planted the crop next to that creek. Just about picking time, the flam'n roos got amongst it. All gone.'

'All?'

'Yeah, apart from a couple of plants.'

'Then, give him his money back!' Jessica was seething.

'Would've, but it's all spent. And, anyway, he didn't want it back,' said they had commitments for the gear.'

'Not an online store, eh.' Jessica with a cynical sneer. 'No returns policy.'

An uncomfortable silence descended across the small room. Harry wondered whether he should just get in the car and drive away from this mess. What did he care about Jessica's brother? A bloody walking disaster!

Harry looked across to Jessica. The look on her face said the same thing, a combination of disbelief and contempt. *So,* he thought, taking a deep breath, *where to from here? Back to Sydney, waiting for Anika, to an abandonment of Jessica's dream of reconciliation, to the realities of living. Simply making a living might be better, forgetting, ignoring the influence of the past, submerged in the demands of the here and now?*

Harry's eyes blurred slightly. He shook his head to clear his vision, suddenly tired, recalling for the first time in days the disjointed, broken conversation with Anika. He felt the prick of dread, the flush of desire, anticipation of their union. Did he have to try, to persist in the face of this chaos? Was any of this worth it? A surge of regret terminated those thoughts; he couldn't abruptly dismiss Jessica's pursuit of some sort of truth.

Yet, now they had the police on their tail!

'So, where's the copper with the gun, now?' Harry said.

'Took off when I grabbed the gun.' Jim smiling. 'Hands around his balls.'

'To where?'

'For reinforcements. Said he was com'n back.'

Shit!

'And what about the rest of the family in town.'

'Just me. I'm the only one they ever dealt with.'

No money, no goods, no hope – Jim was really in the shit!

'You can't go home then, Jim.' Jessica was stating the obvious.

'You could drop me in Cooma.' Jim's pathetic solution.

'They'd find you there in five minutes.' More obvious observations from Jessica.

'Well, Sydney, then.'

'They're from there. They know that ground, you don't, maybe six minutes.' Jessica's grasp of the obvious was wearing thin.

Harry took a deep breath. *There's a lot of heavy breathing going on here*, he thought. *Maybe that's good for thinking, oxygen to the brain.* He hesitated, realising that the solution was part of the obvious, a slice of reason in this confusion. 'You could come with me,' said Harry, feeling the bleakness of the prospect. 'I mean, we could continue to the coast, together, disappear into the hills and forest. Be the best part of a week to walk the distance. Time for things to settle a bit, maybe for them to give up looking for you?'

'They won't give up, Harry.' Jessica holding tenaciously to the obvious.

'Well, it's worth a try. And they're unlikely to follow on foot, not through that country to the coast.'

'And I know some of the old paths between here and The Bay.' Jim's eyes flicked hopefully from Harry to Jessica and back again.

Harry wasn't sure he wanted this solution – *like digging a hole, climbing into it and digging deeper*, he thought.

Yet, he guessed he would need help navigating his way onto the old paths, through the rugged terrain between here and the coast. He just hoped Jim's familiarity with the way wasn't merely an invention to buy time, to save his hide from an ugly mob of crims and coppers.

Chapter 7

Into the Wilderness

August 25

Striding forward, arms pumping, chin held high, Jim looked happy, no longer the mournful creature who had slumped about the cabin. He took in deep drafts of air, great currents that seemed to go on forever, released with reluctance, a proclamation of his triumph over adversity.

Harry struggled to maintain pace with him over the uneven ground, sweat running in torrents down his back, accumulating as pools between shirt and pack. Jim led them into the secret, hidden country, across the divide between the high plateau and the coast, into the forgotten country, along the paths of the first people to the shrouded pass from west to east.

They skirted the edge of a stand of pines, a relic of reckless clear-felling and reforestation before the war, and plunged into the old growth. The wild forest seemed to break like a stormy sea against the ordered development of the plantation, a turbulent tide thwarted by the shadowed calm of the towering conifer cliffs. Harry felt the oppressive mass of the pines recede as they plunged into old woodland. The undergrowth was almost a jungle now without the scorching ministrations of the first people, the forest canopy permitting a dampened, dappled light to play across the scrub-crowded ground. *We'll have to fight our way through this*, he thought as another deluge of sweat flooded his back, *and this pace is going to kill me.*

'If we don't slow down,' he said to Jim's back through gritted teeth, 'I won't make it!' *There is always the four-wheel-drive option*, he thought.

'Great day, isn't it?' said Jim, ignoring Harry's moan, a smile playing across his face as he stopped and turned.

'Yeah, fine,' said Harry. 'It's a great day for walking.'

Harry grabbed his water flask, taking a large swig of the tepid fluid. 'But it's still over a hundred kilometres to the coast, and my legs need a slower pace.'

Jim smiled again. 'Love go'in bush,' he said, clearly suppressing a slight smirk. 'The bastards won't find me in among this.'

'Or my body after I die of exhaustion in this undergrowth.' Harry seriously doubted his ability to reach the coast.

'The path to the pass is just beyond this bloody scrub, through some really nice open bush. My uncle's been burning it back for years like the blackfellas used to do in the old days.'

Harry looked about, peering suspiciously through the tangled undergrowth. He couldn't see the way, couldn't see any route, no way forward, just a wall of foliage, stretching, grasping, scratching branches that would repulse any invasion. "It's a bloody jungle in there,' he said, folding his hands across his shoulders, instinctive protection against a potentially violent enemy.

Jim looked at Harry, silent. *Was it pity or contempt that Harry saw?* A smile eventually appeared – mocking? 'Just a few metres more of this,' said Jim. 'And we'll be clear of it.' Harry confessed to growing scepticism; this was the person who consorted with criminals, with the corrupt, with homicidal maniacs that barked at their heels. How could he trust anything the man said?

'Your uncle come this way often, then?' Harry gazed forlornly at the dense, tangled undergrowth. Harry's mood was darkening.

'Every season, he lights cool fires that don't burn to the forest crown. The way it's been done by the blackfellas for ages.'

'Ages? So, why this?' said Harry, pointing to the glowering wall of spikey branches.

Jim abruptly turned away as he said, 'Yeah, thousands of years. This wall of scrub keeps them whitefellas away from the old paths.' He pushed firmly through the barrier, plunging into the jungle, disappearing as the scrub folded about him.

Harry hesitated a moment, the crack of branches warning of imminent scrapes and scratches, of blood drawn in the name of secrecy – the concealment of what? Harry glanced at his feet, perhaps buying time to convince himself that he possessed the necessary fortitude to complete this task. He needed to follow through, keep up with Jim, or maybe he was just delaying the inevitable, afraid of a few scrapes, a bit of blood?

He lifted his eyes. Jim had disappeared, leaving a few broken twigs in his wake.

Bloody hell!

Déjà vu made him hesitate, a feeling that he had been here before and was destined to meet ancient relics in these mountains, a mood deep within him that had persisted since that day with Gwen. Residues of past lives were likely to endure in the deep forest.

Harry gathered himself. No, he didn't want to be left alone, fated to wander aimlessly in search of mythical paths, barking hounds behind, fear his only companion.

He stepped forward into the break, arms pushing away the grasping foliage, into the unknown. Jim's trail of destruction, broken limbs, crushed leaves, hinted at the way, a path that appeared to be sealed before him slamming shut behind. He stopped, embraced by the caressing scrub, an odd pricking at his scalp. It would be easy to just give up now, lie down, submerging himself in this sea of undergrowth, in nature's cocoon, drifting away to nothingness. He felt his knees begin to buckle, a sinking feeling rising from his feet. His heart beat rapidly; shallow breaths feeding tightness about his temples, blurring vision, nourishing nausea in the pit of his stomach.

Then something hard, vice-like at his elbow!

'Come on!' The words slowly penetrated the haze. 'Come on! We haven't got all day.'

Harry looked at his elbow, then at the face. Jim pulled, Harry lurched forward, an automatic, stumbling response through thick scrub, and then ...

A clearing.

A path?

'Thought I'd lost you there for a moment,' Jim said. 'Couldn't hear you behind me.'

Harry considered his response. What could he say? That he had panicked, had felt like the ground was sucking him down, that he was confused? 'A bit disoriented,' he said.

Silence.

Finally, Jim said, 'Yeah, thick scrub can do that to'y.' Harry could feel the close inspection, then the dismissal.

Harry stamped his feet, shaking away the vestiges of the numbness that had invaded his legs. 'So,' said Harry, leaning forward to peer along the narrow walkway, 'where's this path headed?'

'All the way to the coast, I reckon, though I've never walked it before.'

Harry said nothing. He felt ashamed that he had almost surrendered to the instinct for self-preservation, almost walking away, thinking about his return to the coast, Anika's arrival, intimacy in the quiet seclusion of the beach house, the scent of her hair caressing his face as they drifted into a light, contented slumber, dosing until hunger drove them from the bed. Anika's long legs unfurling as she slipped from under the covers and walking naked to the kitchen for a hot cup of something, it didn't matter what, and hours of idle chat, backs propped against the bedhead, until their bodies, like irresistible lures, joined once again.

'You don't need to go back,' he'd said. 'Bangladesh won't miss you.' Anika didn't respond immediately, didn't need to – Harry understood well her deep desire for connection, delineation of the past with the present, the continuum, the conduit that guided their emotions, beliefs and responses. She was travelling towards a light, a shining star that gave her existence meaning.

Anika lay on the bed, wrapping her legs about his, naked middles moulded, morphing into one. 'I need to do it,' she had said softly.

'Then do it,' he'd said, not really understanding her meaning. 'You have to live.'

'Harry?' Jim stared curiously at Harry. 'We really need to get a shuffle on before we lose too much of the day.'

'Right,' said Harry, shifting his small pack to a more comfortable position on his shoulders.

Jim swung about, striding purposefully once again, body swaying slightly, broad shoulders brushing through the undergrowth that reached expectantly across the path. Harry glanced skyward, catching a glimpse of a dark figure in the forest canopy. Was it a raven? *We're being followed*, he thought, *though not yet, it seems, by Jim's crim mates.*

After a brief pause, Harry bustled along the track after Jim. He didn't want a repeat of his earlier muddle.

*

The pathway – a traditional way for migration and trade, or a trail to nowhere? Jim seemed familiar with every twist and turn, rarely hesitating when faced with a choice, as the narrow track led them into rugged country, some parts precipitous, sheer drops into gorges with rocky foundations, turbulent streams rushing eastward into shaded, arcane forest. Harry settled into a dogged stride close behind Jim, worried that the vagaries of the path would leave him alone, stranded yet again.

Jim stopped abruptly at a junction, Harry almost colliding with his mountainous form. 'Jesus, Jim,' said Harry. 'Some warning, will you.'

'Right, goes down,' Jim said, pointing. 'Left continues along the ridge.' Harry heard the uncertainty in his voice.

'You've been pretty sure where you're going till now. What's the problem?'

'Scarred tree.' Jim walked to the side of the track, laying his hand on the trunk of a large eucalypt, a great gash revealing the tree's interior.

'What? What's that telling you?'

'Decision point. Not just ours, but all them fellas used to come through here.'

'So, what's it saying?'

'Don't know.'

'What do you mean, don't know?' Harry was sceptical. 'You're a blackfella, why don't you know?'

"Cause you whitefellas sent us all off to Wallaga Lake, trashed our culture and taught us about Jesus!'

Harry saw the irritation at his question. *Should have kept my mouth shut,* he thought immediately, then recognised the absurdity of his regret. *If he didn't ask, how would he know?*

The past was like a puzzle with missing pieces. What had happened? Perhaps the Land Council knew, had a grip on the misdemeanours of the past, understood the whole sordid story or at least the significant bits. Harry thought of Jimmy. *How could someone disappear so completely; not fading away, but obliterated, instantly gone, and along with his history, his emotions, his sense of place, maybe the places themselves?* Jessica described her grandfather as a taciturn man, given to unusual exploits, with the courage to stand firm against almost anything. He could see such a person hazarding the trek from the mountains to the sea, at a time when there were no roads through this wilderness, when survival meant knowing the way, living off the land, being free of any need for others. But, Jessica only had scraps, fragments from her grandmother and mother, distorted remnants that must inevitably miss essential parts of the story. Had Jimmy ended his life at Wallaga Lake with the people of this country, broken and disoriented, forgotten amidst the greed and destructive purpose of the invaders?

'Wallaga Lake? Where's that?' said Harry.

'Bermagui,' Jim said. 'They shoved a bunch of us blacks from up here in a settlement on the north side of the lake. Y'know, people from the Monaro, Delegate, Bombala, along with the coastal mob from Twofold Bay and Narooma and in between.'

Harry's thoughts wandered as they trudged along the ridge – Jim had decided on the way. He knew Bermagui, a small, vibrant fishing village against the coast, fringed by tall forest. But the Wallaga Lake aboriginal settlement? Harry couldn't remember any mention of it.

'When did that happen?' said Harry, starting to breathe hard as the path degenerated into boulder-strewn scree.

'They started way back, late eighteen hundreds, I think.'

'What did they do?' Harry displaying his ignorance.

'What do y'mean?' Jim stopped, turned with a quizzical expression. Even he was breathing hard now.

'I mean, why did they ship them all to Wallaga Lake?' Harry hadn't heard any of this history.

'They were a bloody nuisance where they were. The squatters didn't have any use for'em anymore. The blackfellas had shown them all the ways to get from here to there.'

Harry silent.

'Then they started put'n up fences, and the blackfellas couldn't get around freely anymore. All the best land was stolen by the squatters.'

Harry couldn't help seeing the parallel with Anika's stories of her North American forebears: classic gradual dispossession.

'They occasionally knocked off a sheep or a cow or two. So, the bloody squatters went out and shot whole families 'cause of that. And when they were half-starved and couldn't resist anymore, they shipped them out.'

'To Wallaga Lake?'

'Yeah, and other places too. Split up whole families, tribes, fucked up everything.'

Jim returned to the climb, the brow of the hill now in sight, a bald south-facing cliff with an overhang. The drama of the place held Harry in thrall as they mounted the top of the scarp, the sheer fall into the deep ravine, stripped giants perforating the forest crown, the tangled hills grading to light purple in the distant east.

'Reckon I can see the ocean from here.' Harry shaded his eyes with a hand, squinting to the east.

Jim clambered across the broken scree to the overhang. 'On a good day,' he said. 'Y'can almost see bloody New Zealand from here.' He sat heavily atop a pile of broken shards.

Harry looked about the hilltop, down to the turning point, up to the pinnacle of the ridge. 'This the end of the track, then?'

'Yeah, reckon we went the wrong way at the tree.'

'Good view, though.' *It'd be a great place to watch for newcomers,* Harry thought. *Sit here, invisible from all directions, a gatekeeper of sorts.* 'What's at the base of that cliff,' he said, pointing to the ridge.

Jim followed the finger's direction. 'Dunno. Looks like a cave.'

Harry felt the prick of apprehension, an uneasiness that almost made him advise a retreat, back to the tree, into the valley and their scheduled meeting with Jessica. He felt comfort in that thought.

Jim rose to his feet, scrambling unsteadily up the steep incline towards the cliff base, dislodging loose shale fragments as he climbed. 'Come on,' he said as he disappeared over the brow. 'Let's take a look.'

No choice, Jim gone, Harry was forced to follow. A slippery ascent, a curiously smooth summit, signs of tenancy, though not recent occupation, and a crack in the scarp wall. Jim stood quietly at the entrance, hesitant. 'Not sure I can fit through there,' he said, head inclining to the fracture, broad shoulders appearing to inflate. 'But, you could.' A smile.

Harry didn't want to do it. 'It's just a crack in the rocks,' he said. 'There's no cave in there.'

'Sure, there is.' Jim was sceptical. 'Look, there's an old path leading inside.' Harry avoided a glanced at the ground, not wanting to accept the evidence.

'I can't fit through either.'

'Sure, you can. Plenty of room for a small fella like you.'

It was Harry's turn to be sceptical. 'I'm not much smaller than you,' he said, squaring his shoulders.

'Well, fuck it,' said Jim, launching himself sideways at the crack. His body jammed hard against the rock walls – there was no way he could pass through.

Harry stood silently, watching Jim wiggle, shake and twist, grunting with the effort to force an entrance to the imagined heart of the rock. The desperate labour finally ceased. Jim detached from the crack, walking casually to Harry. 'Caught a glimpse of something in there,' he said.

'Bullshit!' Harry wasn't going to be fooled. 'You were like a worm sticking its head out of a hole. You couldn't have seen anything.'

'Yeah. I did.' Jim's face bore the scars of his tussle with the rocks. 'Twisted m'head around, saw a big open space just past this bloody entrance.'

Harry saw the encroachment of the inevitable. His sense of foreboding turned the rock fissure into a crack of doom, a pathway to something more than unpleasant, perhaps life-threatening, certainly life-changing. He stood mute, awaiting the final cut.

'You looked scared, Harry.'

Let it pass.

'Is it the possums or the snakes?'

Harry turned his gaze to the east, letting go of his breath in a rush that made a whistling sound. Was he touching a real vibe or turning into that hyper-imaginative schoolboy?

'Maybe Jessica should be here to do the real work?'

'Yeah, she's a gutsy bird,' said Harry. 'Wanted to go back and find you when it looked like you'd been shot.' Harry ran his tongue across dry lips.

'We're a close family.'

'I talked her out of it.'

'I doubt that. No one tells Jess what to do.'

'I've noticed.'

Jim shuffled his feet, impatience gathering. 'So, are you gunna take a butcher's at this cave?'

Harry was silent as he considered the torn rock, the jagged entry to the unknown. The foreboding hadn't diminished, uncertainty closing about him, holding his feet motionless to the ground.

'Why are you so keen for me to stick my head in there.'

"Cause I reckon this place is important. It's where those fellas, years ago, saw what was going on, could see where they'd come from.'

'Yeah, it's certainly a high point.'

'No, I mean, they could see how the world turned. It's a crossroads. One way to the sea, the other to the mountains. It's a place to sit and think, to record what's happened.'

'Shit, Jim.' Harry felt a slight lifting of the pall that had weighed him down. 'That's deep!'

'No, I just feel it. And I reckon you can feel it too.'

In his mind, Harry could feel the rightness of Jim's words, the sense that this place was special, that it projected an aura of divinity, a demure sacredness firmly embedded in the earth.

'All right,' Harry said. 'Get out of my way. I'll see if I can squeeze through that bloody gap.'

Harry lurched forward into the gap, sliding past the rough walls, into the dimly lit, dank interior, where time faltered, the years withdrawing in the face of a culture that had outlasted ice age and drought – a chronicle, a history, a bible that defined a thousand generations and their submission to the land.

CHAPTER 8

August 25

In the damp dark, uneasy with the unknown, confined on both sides by hard stone walls, Harry shuffled forward, the passage narrowing slightly as he went. Would he have a problem backing out if the way became too tight? He wasn't claustrophobic, but he could never understand how some people actually thought that caving was fun: wriggling into impossibly tight places with little hope of rescue if things went wrong, just for the thrill, the anticipation of finding something; a cave, a hollow in the rock that no one had ever seen or even knew existed. Such an anthropocentric view of the planet.

The corridor narrowed further. *Any more, and I'll have to back out,* he thought, as the light from behind began to fade. The passage turned a little, the rough walls obstructing the feeble light. He pulled a small torch from his pocket, an emergency tool that he always carried – not meant for caving, not really meant for a real emergency either – but a brace against the unknown, strong enough to give some sort of guidance in this gloom.

As he broke through a particularly tight section, expecting yet more jockeying against defiant walls, a brief reflection ahead made him stop. He peered into the dark nothingness, now a slightly larger space, expecting to see an animal – this was undoubtedly an ideal daytime abode for a nocturnal creature.

Nothing.

He waved the light from side to side, hoping to catch a glimpse of a beast.

Nothing.

'Do y'see anything?' Jim's shout was muffled by the dense stone.

'No!' Harry was ready to abandon this stupidity.

'Have you reached the cave?'

Harry was tired of Jim's insistence that there was a cave. 'There's no fucking cave here, Jim. Just bloody darkness!'

'Keep going then. There's got to be.' Why was Jim so sure?

Harry turned back to the void. One more flash of the light before he would definitely back out of this place, return to their trek, and get some measure of sense into what they were doing. He could almost taste the evening wine, feel the soft comfort of a real bed, hear the dulcet tones of Jessica's voice as she questioned them on the day – *uneventful Jess, we just walked the distance*. He swept the beam across the dark space.

Then the world exploded!

Sharp claws, fangs, scrabbling legs, feet, a gaping maw flung him back against the stone, his ears, mind filled with wild, furious screaming.

'Shit!'

And then it was gone as quickly as it had appeared!

'What the fuck was that?' Harry yelled his distress at the distant Jim.

Silence.

'Jim! It was headed towards you. What the fuck was it?'

Silence. Then a faint chuckle reached Harry, mild mirth that grew into uncontained laughter echoing down the passageway.

'Jim, what's so bloody funny.'

The laughter finally abated. 'A cat, a feral bastard the size of a fox, moving so fast it left furrows in the ground.'

Harry gathered his wits, swallowing hard. 'Well, that does it, mate.' Enough was enough, and Harry wanted to move on. 'I'm coming out.'

'No, no, Harry.' An instant retort, firm resolve in Jim's voice. 'If that damn cat was there, then I reckon you're close.'

Harry stood quietly for a moment. Close to what? He couldn't see sense in Jim's words. Why would the location of the *damn cat* provide anything more than evidence of universal stupidity: the importation of cats and their release into the wild by the European invaders? He drew in a deep draft of the dank air, leant heavily against the stone wall, and closed his eyes for a moment.

Shit! What was he doing in this place? What was the point of any of this? It wasn't going to lead anywhere other than to disappointment; maiming or death perhaps, at the whim of vile feral creatures.

Harry rested, back against the wall, his mind churning through all the compelling reasons to abandon this examination of the earth's bowels – arguments for leaving, a million and one. Against? He couldn't think of any, except maybe Jessica.

He took another deep breath, coughing slightly as the dust, stirred by the passing maelstrom, settled into his lungs – *this was rejection*, he thought, *at a cellular level.*

All right, he said to himself as the one reason stuck in his mind, *one last look.* He shook his head in disgust at his gutless submission, swinging the torch once more to the darkness, the beam absorbed for a moment by the emptiness, then, suddenly, scanning across an object, the hint of something tangible in the space, a large chamber.

Was this Jim's goal, his *el dorado*?

He stopped the light's travel, pulling it back across the dusty cave floor, searching for the thing, hunting, hoping for reassurance that this wasn't wasted time, that Jim was right, that this was a place vital to their search.

And there it was! The light rested upon a smooth rock, a pedestal beneath a smoke-blackened ceiling. Harry swept the light across the walls of the cave.

Images!

Dense, colourful, intricate, vibrant. The walls were adorned with millennia of imaginings, the dreams and visions of those who had passed this way from sea to mountain and back. They had followed the seasons, inured to the razor of time.

It took several moments for Harry to recover his equilibrium. Finally, a shout back down the crack, 'I think we've struck gold, Jim.'

'What do'y mean?'

'You'll have to find some way to get in here to take a look.' Harry couldn't drag his eyes from the gallery.

*

Jim writhed, squirmed and grunted his way along the narrow passage, several times wedging so tightly against the walls that Harry thought both their lives would be forfeited – forever entombed in this subterranean gallery. Jim struggled forward, never forsaking the goal, never admitting defeat.

Harry watched, concern growing as Jim forced his way forward. He finally abandoned surveillance of Jim in favour of the wondrous exhibit. The images had a clear schedule, some scenes partially overlayed by more recent representations, others almost entirely obliterated by the latest – animals in abundance, kangaroos, emus, dingoes, people in various poses, hunting, assembling, meeting. The display paraded deep into the cavern, and Harry followed the pictorial trail.

Until ...

The cave ended in a solid wall.

Harry swung the torch from left to right, across the flat rock surface that towered above him, the vaulted summit fading into the shadows above. He stopped the scan as more images appeared, celestial, stretching gloriously across the broad rampart. Harry leant forward, arm outstretched, fingers longing to feel the glory, aching to explore the intricacies, to be submerged in the heavens.

'Harry, don't touch!'

Hand almost touching the wall, Harry half-turned. 'You made it,' he said. 'Couldn't watch anymore. Reckoned you might be stuck there forever.'

'Nah. Had a crap before I started. Wouldn't have made it full of shit.'

Harry chuckled. 'Jim, you're always full of shit. How would one crap make a difference?'

They both laughed, the mirth echoing through the cavern.

'What *is* this?' Harry waved the light across the canvas.

'It's the emu,' said Jim.

'The emu?' Harry glanced across the wall. 'Yeah, I see it. It's there,' he said, pointing. 'And again, over there. And it's changing.'

'Yeah, changing with the seasons. Running there, after the ladies, there on the nest with the eggs, the fella emus look after the chicks.'

'The seasons?'

'The emu's in the milky way. Told them old folk what the season was, when to head up to the mountains, when to head back to the coast, what food was around.'

Harry slowly moved the torch along the breathtaking image. 'When was this made?' he said.

'Long time ago,' Jim said, then suddenly snatched the torch from Harry's hand, playing the beam onto a series of pictures to the far right. 'Maybe not so long ago. Look!'

Harry peered along the torch beam – a horse, rider, what looked like a stick, perhaps a rifle slung casually across a shoulder. 'Looks like a soldier,' said Harry. Maybe it was a trooper, police that enforced dubious laws that maligned the local people in the colony's early days?

He moved closer – the colours were more vibrant than the surrounding images – a different artist, different materials, a different time, perhaps more recent?

'The rider's wearing a hat.' Jim at the wall now, closely examining the rider. 'A slouch hat!'

Harry felt the shock of recognition – this wasn't just any rider. 'It's a Light Horseman, and look,' he said pointing, as the shockwave reached the tips of his fingers. 'At the figures lying flat in front of the horse.'

Silence, finally broken by Jim's voice, quiet, hushed, reverent. 'My grandfather.' The statement had a finality, a tone that almost suggested veneration. Harry said nothing – the moment demanded respect, reflection, quiet.

Harry held the torch beam steady on the image as the silence extended, swinging the light slowly to the right, to a small alcove – more pictures!

A stride forward to the entrance of the recess, Harry peered into a space crammed with pictures; images that took the breath from his lungs. He recoiled at their graphic ferocity.

'Jesus,' he said.

'What?' A question from behind.

The words would not come. Harry felt the author's torment, the pain, understood the privacy of this place, was loath to violate an intensely private revelation.

'Take a look for yourself,' Harry said, backing away, handing the torch to Jim.

Jim pushed through the narrow entrance, his bulk blocking the flashlight beam in the small hollow. Harry sagged against the smooth cave wall, slowly letting his legs fold until he rested on the sandy floor, enfolded by the dark of a lightless cave. Harry's understanding was that his grandfather, Eiric, had returned from the war in Palestine with few regrets, noble in intent and deed, gallant in triumph, and that seemed to be supported by all the evidence.

The images, though …

What were they saying? Were they the product of a deranged mind? Or did they tell another truth – a more private truth that described the reality of war?

'It's him all right.' The flashlight swept across Harry.

'How do you know?'

'"Cause it can't be anyone else. Come, and I'll show ya.'

'Jim, I won't fit in there with you.'

'Yeah, you will; it's bigger than y'think.'

Harry followed Jim's bulk, bent low into the painted chamber, dreading Jimmy's window on the past, his exposé of misdemeanours, the transgressions of war and its consequence.

The images stretched the length of the alcove's wall, ten metres at least, crudely drawn but lively – there was no doubt about the theme, about the emotion in the rendition: horses, at full gallop, men fighting men, men trampled by rampant horses, burning buildings, chaos, mayhem; and to the side, almost an afterthought image, a horse, prone, the same slouch hat standing above the animal.

'What's that in his hand?' Harry craned forward, almost touching the image with his finger.

'A stick,' Jim said, then changing his mind, 'Ah, no, I reckon it's a gun.'

'He's shooting the bloody horse!' Harry found it shocking; he didn't quite know why. The whole painted scene was disturbing, redolent with chaos and death; the revelations of a troubled mind, the release of memory or the purging of guilt?

'Is this your grandfather?' Harry had to know.

'Not sure, but look here.' Jim said. 'I reckon that's a prayer tower, like the ones they have in them Muslim countries.'

An image from Harry's time in North Africa, Bangladesh, passed through his mind – the illustration was crude, but the provenance was unmistakable. 'So, what's it doing here?'

Jim shook his head.

The cave was plunged into darkness.

*

Harry could never understand the alignment of things, how events seemed to synchronise, dovetailing one with the other, matching time, location, mood. He could speculate that there were superior forces at work, powers that manipulated mere mortals into streams, events forming a flood that swept everything into the torrent leading to some pre-ordained nexus. His understanding of the cosmos, though, was rudimentary. Some might say it was witless; but repeatedly, he seemed to be placed at the centre of things: the brief connection with his grandfather, the strange appearance of the horse in the desert at the Masada fort in Israel, conversations with Anika that set his mind thinking on the influence of the past, meeting Jessica and her mother, a relationship that put him on the course to this place. And this place, undiscovered, undisturbed for so many years, only to succumb to his intrusion.

Now, bathed in the utter blackness of the cavern, he wondered what coincidences awaited him now.

'The fucking battery's flat.' Jim's frustration boiled over into a shout.

'It's only an emergency torch,' Harry said into the darkness. 'There's only a couple of hours in it.' In the blackness, he heard Jim's feet scrabbling across the floor. 'So, how do we get out of here. You're going to find it hard to go back the way you came in.'

A vision of a desiccated Jim trapped in the darkness, dying by slow degrees, crossed his mind.

More scraping, then boots across the cave floor.

'Not a problem. Follow me.' Jim's voice oozed confidence.

'How can I follow you, you toe rag,' said Harry. 'I can't see you, don't know where you are and anyway, going back the way we came in won't do you any good.' *And perhaps me as well,* he thought.

'We're not going that way.'

'What do you mean? We're going to walk through stone walls or something?'

'Sort of.' The reply came from further away in the dark.

'Jim! I can't see you. Where are you going?' Harry stood rigid in the blackness. Which way was he going?

Silence.

Shit! Where to turn? Harry felt panic rising. The bastard was abandoning him. He'd be the one to end his days as a waterless, shrunken corpse in the bowels of the earth if he couldn't find the entrance. Jim had an escape route; Harry would need to try his luck at their entry point – he didn't like the odds for an escape that way.

Harry drew a breath, ready to shout an accusation into the void.

A vice clamped about Harry's arm.

'Come on y'tosser. This way.'

Stumbling, Harry was pulled through the thick night. Was this how the blind lived in a sunny world, reliant on vague senses, on others as guides?

Thankfully, the cavern floor was relatively smooth and level. Once he stabilised himself, Harry had no trouble keeping pace with Jim – as long as he maintained contact with Jim's broad back, arm outstretched. He could hear Jim's breath ahead, increasingly laboured as the ground started to tilt slightly upward – the pressure of the climb in his thighs.

The gradient suddenly became precipitous – almost to the point where Harry thought he would need to drop his hands to the ground. The cave floor was rough now, tumbling rocks making progress slow, feet searching for purchase amongst the loose scree.

Harry stopped, suddenly realising that the blackness had turned to gloom. They were in a tight passage – ahead, the soft light of a westering sun filtered into the low-roofed tunnel, Jim's bulk now shadowed against the light.

The last few metres were hard going, almost a vertical climb. Ahead, Jim scaled the jagged ascent disappearing over the crest. Harry clambered desperately to the top, pushing through thick foliage that crowded the entrance to the tunnel, looking around as he emerged.

'Just above where we went in,' he said. 'How did you know this was here?'

'Didn't, wasn't sure.' Jim triumphant. 'But I saw a worn path in the cave before your bloody torch carked it.'

'In the dark. How did you know the way?'

'Didn't,' Jim said, turning away, ready to go – the conversation ended it seemed – then stopped, turning back to face Harry, pressing his index finger against his nose. 'We blackfellas automatically know the way around our sacred places.'

Harry stood silent, impressed, thinking through the implications of Jim's admission. 'You felt the way?'

Jim's face broke into a broad grin. 'Nah, all I felt was the breeze coming from here, down the tunnel. Knew if I kept head'n into it, we'd find some sort of way out.'

Bloody lucky to find it, Harry thought, *but maybe it wasn't just luck?*

'What are we going to do about what we've found,' said Harry. 'It's all pretty significant."

Jim's face turned grim. 'Do about it? We do noth'n, say noth'n. Moment we tell people, they'll be hordes of the bastards up here. Before y'know it, they'll have visitor centres and restaurants selling tickets to see it. No, we say noth'n.'

'But your grandfather's paintings ...'

'We say noth'n to nobody.' Jim's forbidding threatened to turn fierce.

'Right'yo then,' Harry said, moving towards the trail. 'Let's get to our rendezvous with Jessica.

Fine, Harry thought, *but what he had seen changed everything, and Jessica had a right to know.*

The last of the trek passed for Harry, in a dream: around Mt Imlay to the highway where Jessica waited impatiently for their arrival: pacing anxiously along the road, from car to the trail and back again; she had promising leads and wanted to explore them.

95

CHAPTER 9

August 27

S nowy Curlew was a blithe person: blithe with his clothes, blithe with his language, blithe with his gestures, maybe even blithe with his thoughts. Jessica had ferreted out the old bloke, *a refugee*, Harry thought, from society and everything civilised. Her dogged determination to turn every stone, to learn everything she could from as many sources as possible led her into very peculiar crevasses. Snowy had lifted his head above the parapet, was caught and corralled.

He pushed the map across the table. 'Been up there,' he said. 'It's just a fucking ruin.'

Harry leant forward, peered at the chart, pointing a finger. Snowy was right, of course – he'd been living in these hills for probably a century or more, or so it was rumoured. And Jessica had been right too. In her view, the most recent images on the cave walls were a message; her grandfather wanted to leave a note for future generations.

The discovery of their objective was more luck than design; Harry's memory had been cajoled, teased, bludgeoned into submission by Jessica's will. Harry still didn't understand how that worked.

'Just like those who left those cave paintings so many years ago,' she said. 'He was following a tradition. Only this time, he specifically wanted us to know how devastating war was, how so many lives were destroyed, whether they died on the battlefield or not, whether they were human or not.'

The revelation was disturbing: violence, the trail of blood across the series of illustrations, broken bodies, the bleak final dispatch of the horse.

'Grandma Gurley said he loved his horse, loved him like a brother, spent hours talking to him. She reckoned the horse talked back, in a way only Jimmy could hear.'

'Then, why is he shooting his friend?'

'They couldn't bring the horses home. The British refused to foot the transport bill. So, the men took matters into their own hands. They'd seen the bad way the Arabs treated their horses, and risked court-marshal, so, they went out and shot them rather than leave them behind. The Australian government were so gutless, they didn't support the men.'

'A colonial mindset, I guess. Still part of the empire', said Harry, as if that was sufficient to explain the sadness, the violence, the blood. Everything.

'My grandfather never forgave himself. Shooting a friend like that pretty much broke him.' Jessica's explanation was delivered without rancour, but Harry could feel the sorrow.

So, where does this get us, thought Harry. *We suspect Jessica's grandfather came this way, but we've not got any actual proof. Just a few scrappy drawings on a cave wall, perhaps made by someone connected to the Great War. Now what?*

'I reckon there's a clue somewhere in all those drawings,' said Jessica. She almost seemed to read Harry's mind.

'Clue to what?' Harry said, instantly regretting his response. He needed to discard that innate scepticism.

'Where he was headed next, of course.' Jessica held firmly to her beliefs. 'It's him, Harry. I believe it. Jim believes it. You should too. It's all more than just coincidence.'

'So, where's that then?'

Jessica silent for a moment, eyes rolling in thought, tongue moving delicately over lips. 'Think through all the paintings on the wall,' she said. 'there's got to be a clue to his next step.'

Harry couldn't see it, couldn't isolate the images from each other in his mind, the chaos from the blood, the emotion from the message. Eyes closed, he gradually forced his memory to the first glimpses, the initial illumination, past the shock of the discovery. He trawled along the wall, recalling a boat upon an ocean, four-legged animals that looked vaguely like camels, long lines of horses passing by shattered buildings, the dead piled high in a ravine, horses at full gallop, scattered, torn and dismembered bodies. His memory arrived at a man standing above a horse, legs astride, clearly braced against a final mortal act.

'No,' he said, after a moment, eyes open. 'I can't remember anything that might be a clue.'

'Try again,' Jessica said, desperation creeping into her voice.

'Jim might remember more,' he said. He wanted to be free of this inquisition.

'Try!' Jessica impatient now, her voice almost a shout. "Jim can't remember what he had for breakfast, far less things like this!'

Harry obliged. Better to comply than suffer Jessica's harsh recrimination.

The final scene again. He was set on the tragedy, focused on Jessica's explanation, Jimmy's predicament: the ultimate abandonment of a friend, a confidante that had supported him through a bitter war.

Harry scanned the scene within his mind. No, there was nothing more, no messages, no subtle pointers, no signs that could satisfy Jessica's thirst for answers to her anxiety, to her self-doubt.

He drifted for a moment, letting the colours, the hues, the shadows of the cave wash about him. The damn flashlight! What had he missed because of its failure, his negligence in not having a backup light?

Then ...

There it was!

Small. At the periphery of his vision.

A mountain!

A mountain, shaped like a pyramid, and halfway up towards the peak, the crude rendition of a house.

'Just past the last image,' Harry said, opening his eyes again. 'Almost in the shadows. Something that looks like a mountain, a triangle, or a pyramid, and a house or cabin near the top.'

Jessica smiled. 'I knew it!'

'Knew what?'

'That he'd leave something for us to follow. It's either Mount Imlay near Eden or Mount Dromedary near Bermagui.'

How could she know that? Harry couldn't suppress his incipient scepticism.

'And I know just the person who can show us the way.' Jessica was triumphant.

She always had contacts. Harry looked at the old man. Snowy smiled: a curiously benign smile for someone so irascible.

'How do we get there?' Jessica said, pushing the map towards Snowy with the flat of her hand.

Snowy remained silent for a moment, chewing his gums. His teeth had seen better days, and most had been consigned to oblivion many years ago. 'Y'can walk up from Tilba, a steep path but short, or there's a logging track y'can drive on, but that's a long way 'round.'

'Show us the road on the map.' Jessica was now inclined to the dictatorial.

Snowy pulled the chart back towards him, leaning over to examine the grid, finally tracing a line with his bent arthritic finger.

*

August 31
Afternoon

'Turn left at the next junction,' said Harry.

Jessica slowed the car, steering carefully to avoid the gravel piled against the track shoulder – a logging trail, recently graded to smooth, the remnant winter corrugations gone. The vehicle slowed as it turned into a steep, narrow path, climbing immediately towards the summit through dense forest crowding about the route – a walking track rather than a road. The late afternoon shadows from the trees spread their fingers across the path, at times confusing the way.

Harry glanced sideways as they climbed, over the sheer drop to the valley, then at Jessica's hands, white-knuckled on the steering wheel. *Don't let go*, he thought, as the nose of the car dipped violently into an erosion channel. Jessica's old car heaved sideways, closer still to the abyss.

'Can this old buggy make it?' Harry said as the vehicle bucked again, the ancient suspension tested to its limit.

'It's not the car,' Jessica said as the vehicle bucked again. 'It's the bloody tyres. They needed changing before this, and I'll definitely need new ones now.'

Images of shredded tyres, buckled rims, a pitiful three-wheeled old car stranded next to a precipice dominated Harry's thoughts as he clung to the tired seat – *too many bums have been perched here*, he thought. 'Snowy said the hut was about halfway up,' he said.

Another sharp jolt rattled his teeth.

'We should be almost there.' Was that wishful thinking? Jessica was breathless as she fought with the steering wheel.

Harry braced himself for the next wild gyration, unsure how many more of these violent convulsions he could take. Then suddenly, they hurtled onto a patch of unobstructed sunshine, lurching across a rare, smooth section of road, through an opening in a decrepit fence-line, into a large clearing fringed with dense, luxuriant forest, tall trees, ferns crowding about their bases.

Jessica abruptly released the car from its labours, ominous groaning from suspension now the dominant sound. Harry wasn't convinced it was only the tyres that needed attention.

'We're here, I think,' he said, scanning the open ground. 'Look!'

A tumbledown structure lay barely above the ground at the far side of the glade. Jim's hunch had paid off, Jessica had proved that persistence could be rewarded, Snowy had shown the way. Harry suffered the burden of his doubt. In the fading light of another day, here was the culmination of their faith, the divine commitment; he immediately felt the significance of the place. Was this where Jimmy had ended his days, secluded in a mountain forest, deserted, forsaken by the people he had tried to support, by the community, the nation, the world?

The car door squealed: Jessica tumbled from the car. She gathered herself, striding purposefully across the open ground towards the ramshackle building.

'Wait!' Harry felt a blackness rising from the distant ruin.

Jessica hesitated. 'What?'

'I'm not sure about that place.'

'Don't be ridiculous!'

Yes. Don't be ridiculous. Harry, the unbeliever, was advising caution over some sort of spooky feeling. How could he support such a feeling?

Jessica returned to the task, striding forward once again.

'Wait!' Harry shouted the warning. The feeling had intensified.

Jessica stopped, turned to face the vehicle, obvious irritation. 'What, Harry, we're almost there. This is it. I can feel it in my bones!'

Harry regarded the collapsed cottage that rose behind a defiant Jessica, the structure almost merging with the deep forest as the day joined with the evening – abandoned, unremarkable, benign. How could there be anything sinister in that view, any malevolence or nascent treachery lingering about the place? Harry shook his head: was Mr Unbeliever proclaiming that evil spirits were afoot?

Ridiculous!

And yet ...

Harry peered closer at the edge of the forest. Was that movement in the deepening gloom?

The waft of an evening breeze touched his face. *Imagination,* he thought. The treetops were suddenly rustled against the air drainage from the coast to the east.

Imagination – it could be an unsettling thing, especially in unfamiliar places.

'What is it, Harry?' Harry suddenly realised Jessica was still waiting for an explanation. He felt embarrassed, shook his head again, prepared for a denial, wanting to put this quest back on the rails, bid farewell to disbelief, let the pursuit of their goal resume. *Go,* he thought. *It's just my imagination running riot. Go, find the ultimate truth.*

'What is it, Harry?' Her voice was softer this time. Jessica's irritation changed to hesitation, then to a reversal – she marched back to where Harry stood at the car, frozen by indecision.

'I don't know,' he said as she approached. 'There's something about those ruins. And, I thought I saw something moving behind that fallen stone wall.'

Jessica held him with a fixed stare. 'What sort of movement?'

'It could have been the wind,' he said.

Jessica hesitated, a slight enquiring angle to her head. 'There's no wind, Harry.' Harry glanced upward at the sky, at the motionless trees, the trees silhouetted against the westering sun: Jessica was right. He could have sworn there was wind there only moments ago.

Silence.

Decision.

'Let me go first,' Harry said. Jessica backed away, just a few steps.

'No, I need to see.'

'Listen, Jessica, if there's something in there, then we may need to get out of here in a hurry. And I can run fast.'

'What could it be, Harry. We're not in the wilds of Africa or something, and nothing around here eats people?'

How could he explain this feeling?

'Not that, Jessica. But it's something.' No, now he felt like a real alarmist, an overexcited schoolboy.

Jessica snorted. 'Is this a conversion on the road, Harry? Your submission to the dark side?'

'No, just a feeling.' He couldn't keep the umbrage from his voice.

Jessica silent for a moment, stare still fixed on Harry. Their eyes met, and he saw genuine concern. 'Might be,' he said. 'It's a strong feeling.'

'Doesn't mean it's bad,' she said.

'It's not friendly.' Harry could feel his mind drifting away to the ruin. 'And it's trying to stop me.' He hesitated. 'Stop me from going in, into that broken-down pile of rocks.'

'Why?' Jessica threw her hands wide, exasperated. 'Why would anything want to stop us from going in there?'

Harry had no answer. Jessica clearly didn't expect any. She half-turned towards the broken building a couple of times, silent, biting her bottom lip – so close and now this!

'All right. What do you want me to do?' Jessica, it seemed, was not inclined to challenge the spirits.

'Stay with the car, keep the motor running.' It was the xenophobic approach, but he felt more confident this way if he had to run. 'So, if you see me running out of there, we can bugger off real quick.'

Jessica just nodded her head. Silent, she pushed past Harry, striding back to the car. 'Call me if things are fine in there.'

Harry watched her go, then turned to face the sullen ruin, ambling into the long shadows of the tall forest, trees now silhouetted black against the sinking sun. He glanced briefly skyward. The first stars burst into a sky, submitting to dark purples, colours grading to deep green. *It is intriguing,* he thought, *how the world kept turning despite all the machinations of man, despite the traumas, the horrors of the past.*

With an effort, he refocused on the ruin, holding back a feeling of dread that seemed to build as he approached the broken, cracked wall – no roof, a remnant door, a pile of rubble exposing parts of the interior. He climbed over the mound, entering uncertain territory. Was it Jimmy who resisted their advance, or some dark power wanting to thwart an understanding of the past, or was it just the product of an overactive imagination?

Harry ducked past a grasping vine, plunging into a dark realm.

107

CHAPTER 10

DISCOVERY

August 31
Early evening

The building was a ruin, fallen roof, crumbling walls, the floor littered with broken timber and scattered stone. Rampant plants, freed from care, embraced the broken parapets, squeezing precipitated moisture from the rock, sending whispering tendrils into dark fissures vacated by ancient mortar. At the end of the forlorn space, exposed to the last of the day's light, rubble crowded about a broken bench, the legs at one end collapsed to form a crude triangle against the floor.

Outside the house, a car waited, the motor still running. Harry could feel the faint chug of the engine and exhaust fade as he moved within the thick stone walls. He walked cautiously to the table. This place had a sense, unfriendly perhaps as if it resented his intrusion, a bitterness that set him on edge – his legs readied to run.

The call of a bird made him look up at the sparse stars in an indigo sky, growing darker as the sun disappeared below the mountains to the west. More pinpoints of light popped into view as he watched.

Harry returned his gaze to the darkening room. If anything was to be learned from this place, he needed to search before the sunlight completely disappeared. A swift march to the end of the room, rummaging through the fallen wreckage, masonry clanging against the hard-packed dirt floor. What did he expect to find? Anything would do – anything that might support this quest, this search for the truth.

A hole appeared in the rubble, a small, dark void that grew as he removed the heavy stone blocks, a passage perhaps to another world, a world of reconciliation, of understanding, the explanation of so many things?

Harry ceased his frantic clawing, stood upright for a moment, stretching his aching back, waiting, maybe, for something to emerge from the blank, gaping maw that descended into fathomless darkness.

Silence – except for the whisper of a light breeze through the ruin and the distant caw of a crow beseeching its mate to come to bed before the night made it too late.

A moment's hesitation, Harry plunged his hand, an arm to the shoulder into the hole – would the serpent strike? Would this be his final reckless act, the rash deed of a fool?

Nothing.

He scrabbled with his fingers, feeling for the extremity, still expecting the sting of the viper.

Nothing.

Harry relaxed his arm, flexing fingers to release the tension as he prepared to withdraw his arm. This had been a slim chance, a rumour that had grown in his mind to embrace certainty. The belief was that they would find evidence of their past in this wreck of a house. Now, inevitably, it had come to nothing, just as everything to date had led to blind alleys and disappointment.

Where to now? he thought. *Could he return to the aimless confusion of his former life, the expectations of others, their disapproval?*

He sighed, rolling almost onto his back as he pulled his shoulder from the opening, his fingers still announcing their need for freedom. He felt the rough walls of the hole as he withdrew, a sudden tight spot grabbing at his sleeve and then ...

It was like an electric shock – fingers scrabbling against the sensation, yet desperately hunting again for the same feeling. Finally, Harry stopped moving, his vision narrowing to a pinpoint, mind imaging the contours of the hole. He searched down to the side, carefully withdrawing his arm once again.

Just my imagination, he thought. *My eagerness for something, anything that might mean we're on the right track.*

Still, his fingers denied defeating its chance.

Inch by inch, eyes closed, Harry continued his careful examination, the rough walls tearing at his fingertips, sensitivity turning to pain as they shredded. Then, he felt it again.

What was it? Soft, yielding, warmth a contrast to the obstinate cold of the stone, cloth against the skin of his arm, hand, fingers. Harry grasped desperately at the object, gathering the loose material until it filled his hand.

Then he pulled – a sudden tug.

Nothing moved.

Despite the chill of the evening air, sweat rolled down his temple, dripping irritatingly into his eyes.

He stopped for a moment, clinging still to the limp shreds in the hole, dug into his pocket with his free hand and wiped his brow with one of the tissues that seemed to breed negligently in the depths of his trousers.

Why don't I invest in some good old-fashioned cloth snot rags? he thought as the tissue dissolved against his brow. *Unhygienic, maybe, but at least they would absorb some of this bloody sweat.* He heard the damp fall of the tissue as he threw it to the side.

A deep breath, trying to slow his heart rate, reducing the tension that made his arms and legs ache.

Attention returned to the object, deep in the hole.

Another sharp pull added strength this time. Finally, some give – another heave!

Still, the object would not budge.

He looked up as he paused, preparing himself for the ultimate effort, his eyes fixed on the crumbling doorway to the room. The approaching winter twilight gloom created a grainy image, the scene now in deep shadow. Suddenly, he had the impression of movement, the slight shifting of the shadows against the fallen block-work.

Shit! Someone was there, someone or something watching.

'Hello!' Harry's voice choked in the dust stirred from the floor. Silence.

Nothing. Then, a flicker of movement resolved into something Harry thought he recognised.

'Jessica, I thought you were going to stay with the car.'

Silence – the form dissolved into the shadows.

Harry had a feeling, premonition entangled with fear, curiosity overwhelmed by dread. The shadows seemed to seethe, roiling like a mist against rising air, blackness crawling unctuously up the broken stone walls.

'Jessica?' Harry said, shaking his head to clear the fog that threatened to creep across his eyes.

A sudden urgency gripped him as he peered into the half-light. He yanked hard on the object within the hole, it broke free, almost tumbling from his grip, wrenched his arm from the pit, on his feet and through the door, expecting whip and lash and bite as he fought through the narrow exit, arms flailing against an anticipated onslaught.

He broke free of the building, running into open ground strewn with the debris from the dismembered building, night's dominion now ascendant. How long had he been inside the building? He saw the car, lights ablaze, the motor still running – it couldn't have been more than ten minutes! Yet, it felt like hours!

He reached the car, desperately gripped the handle, flung open the door, and shouted, 'Get moving! NOW!

'What?'

'NOW!'

The car lurched forward before he could latch the door, throwing him hard against the seatback, pressing air from his lungs. He sat mute, holding tight to the door handle, as the vehicle careered down the rough track, fish-tailing in the loose gravel, through a broken fence line, onto a sealed road in the valley several kilometres from the ruin.

'What was that about? said Jessica.

Harry breathed deeply, considering his reply. He didn't want to appear hysterical. 'There was someone ... or something in the hut,' he said. 'Something malign, didn't want me there, didn't want me to leave.'

'What sort of thing?' Jessica glanced briefly sideways at Harry.

'Don't know.' Harry felt foolish. 'It was in the shadows.'

Jessica, silent, as she slowed the vehicle – the precincts of a small town.

'I thought it was you at first,' Harry said. Maybe that would moderate his aura of panic.

Jessica silent. She glanced sideways again at his hands, now folded in his lap.

'What's in the package?' she said.

'What?' Harry broke himself from reverie, from the hypnotic influence of the white line on the road.

'In your hands. The black package?' The car slowed almost to a halt as they entered the hotel parking area.

Harry looked down, an object wrapped loosely in a faded, stained black cloth, clasped in torn and bleeding fingers.

'I don't know,' he said. 'I found it in the old hut.' He considered the object for a moment. 'I don't think it wanted to come with me.' He shuddered as he remembered the hostile atmosphere in the ruin.

Jessica sat for a moment, then reached across to the back seat, hefting a small first-aid pack.

'Well,' she said, opening the driver's door. 'We can take a look once I've patched up those fingers before they smear blood on everything.'

She walked away to the hotel.

Harry remained seated, watching Jessica walk towards the accommodation. *So much effort getting this far,* he thought, *and just this pathetic little package to show for it. No wonder she seems so disinterested.*

Door open, he levered himself stiffly from the seat, rubbery legs staggering to the hotel entrance.

*

Harry was drowning, a colossal wave breaking above him, holding him down, roaring in his ears, blotting out the sun. How long had he been down now? Surely, he was close to the end!

Something, someone in his head, was saying, 'Are you ready? Get yourself together!'

He woke, room lights blazing, the glare making him squint. His shoulder hurt, a hand reflexively reaching to cradle the joint as he sat upright. His mind was momentarily blank, puzzled. Then he remembered his rush to exit the old hut, his shoulder colliding with the jagged stonework.

He sat upright, shoeless feet fixed to the lino floor, face fastened between hands. When he finally lifted his head, he saw his left-hand fingertips, bound and taped, dark blood staining the cloth. Jessica had done an excellent job – his shredded fingers were at least safe from further harm.

Harry rose cautiously from the couch and walked slowly to

the bathroom, discarding his clothes as he went. The shower beat against him, forcing a sigh of relief. He looked down at a stream of bright red snaking lazily towards the drain near his feet – his fingertips the well-spring. Jessica's ministrations had not completely staunched the flow.

He pulled on an old T-shirt and a pair of jocks whilst heading for the small kitchen, his stock of beer and something to eat. When he entered the sitting room, Jessica was sitting on the settee amid the debris of his discarded clothing.

'Jeez, you're quiet,' he said. 'Didn't hear you come in.'

'Learnt it from my mum. She always used to say I was the noisy one, though.' Jessica pulled the tab on one of Harry's cans of beer.

'Thought I was down one of those,' said Harry pointing to the can.

'Thirsty work driving a car, rescuing panicked whitefellas from ghosts, binding up their wounds, putting them to bed with a bedtime story.'

For a moment, Harry stood silent, remembering when they had arrived, the peculiar, mind-numbing exhaustion he had felt as he entered the room. Jessica had immediately focused on binding the fingers of his left hand, then boiling the jug for a redemptive brew – that done, she pointed to the small package still clasped in Harry's right hand. 'Shall we see what's in it?'

Harry confused. Jessica pointed again. 'In that … or is it secret?' She smiled.

Harry suddenly realised that he had maintained a tight grip on his find from the ruin. He looked vacantly at the prize for a minute, then pushed it forward to Jessica. 'You'd better do the honours. I don't think my fingers are up to it.'

Jessica carefully retrieved the package from Harry's extended hand, turning it slowly as if looking for a way in.

'There's a string and bow holding it together,' Harry said.

'Yeah, I can see that,' said Jessica. 'Just looking for anything else that might tell us something.'

'It's been under a pile of rubble, probably for years. Can't imagine anything surviving on the outside.'

'Y'never know.' Jessica, the eternal optimist.

'And whatever's inside has probably been saturated and destroyed as well.' Harry, the undying pessimist.

Jessica finally pulled the string free. The cloth wrapping seemed to hug closer, tighter, a protective casing. 'Oilskin,' said Jessica.

'Pretty dry,' said Harry. 'It's been there a while.'

Jessica placed the package on the coffee table, plucking delicately at the corners of the wrap. 'Doesn't seem to want to come apart.'

'Maybe, if we just shake it,' Harry said, reaching forward to grab the article.

A hand snaked out, deflecting his grab. 'Patience, Harry.'

Careful dissection resumed.

Finally, slowly peeling back the oilskin, Jessica lifted the cover to reveal the mouldy jacket of a book, a musty smell assailing the nose, making Harry recoil slightly. 'Like opening an Egyptian tomb,' he said. 'We'll probably die now of some horrible, mysterious disease.'

'It's just old.'

Jessica cautiously picked up the book from the oil skin wrap,

Harry half expecting it to disintegrate in the effort – but it held. She lifted the cover and started to read …

Harry sat quietly for a time, as Jessica turned pages, occasionally muttering to herself, finally looking up at Harry, saying, 'Well, I think, after all this time, we have something, Harry.'

'What? What sort of thing is something?' Harry's credulity had been tested so much that he doubted the credibility of anything.

'Best you read it, but I reckon this is his diary.'

'Diary? I didn't know that Jimmy could read, far less write lengthy tomes about his life.'

'You are a whitefella prick, sometimes, Harry. Just because Jimmy was black didn't mean he wasn't educated, couldn't read and write.'

'Yeah, well, why do you think it's Jimmy's writing.'

'Because he's signed the first page and mentioned Grandma Gurley and mum.'

The day had been long; Harry needed time to digest this advent, the beginning of something new, the reward it seemed for their patience, persistence and dedication; the end, he hoped, of his uncertainty.

Harry shook his head, finally focusing on Jessica, seated languidly on the sofa as she sipped another draught from the beer can. 'We'd better get on with reading Jimmy's book, then.'

'Everything in its time, mate,' said Jessica smiling. 'First, you need to get some gear on. You're hanging out all over the place.'

Harry turned in search for some measure of decency and his clothes.

CHAPTER 11

August 31
Evening

The discovery of the book confused Harry, the luck of the find, the malign aura of the ruin, the very existence of such a journal. Nothing had been said about Jimmy that even remotely suggested the man would have kept a diary, least of all one detailing his steps in the wilderness that was his life.

'It's a bit disjointed,' Jessica said, disappointment in her voice.

'That's what diaries are,' said Harry. 'A jumble of thoughts. Anything that pops into the mind.'

'I expected more of a timeline. But it jumps around. And a lot of it. The people, the places, the names are foreign to me.'

'Such as?'

Jessica leafed carefully back through the pages. 'Like ... ummm, this. It's a place I think. Al Auja.' She continued to slowly turn pages. 'And this ... Samakh.'

'Palestine.' Harry reached for the book. 'They're places that were fought over during the First World War. I drove past Samakh when I visited Israel. It's on the shores of the Sea of Galilee.'

Jessica looked thoughtful, reluctantly relinquishing the volume. 'Jimmy's descriptions are ... disturbed is probably the best way to describe them.' Her eyes reflected a deep empathy, worry that Harry wanted to understand.

Harry felt the weight of the journal in his hands, the rough board cover, the old, yellowed paper threatening to disintegrated against careless fingers. The neat writing was faded in places, with a looping flourish that suggested to Harry the author's reluctance to finish each word, a need to hold on to the moment, perhaps to delay abandonment of the memory, the mood? Harry could feel Jessica's gaze as he scanned a few pages.

Gaza. Warrumbungles. Cairo. Horse. Buralga. Names, places, people were jumbled into the narrative, some with greater emphasis, the impression of the pen still forming a deep groove in the paper.

'What made him write all this down?' said Harry as he turned the book in his hands, examining its bulk. 'Not really a natural act for a stockman, is it?'

'Mum always said Jimmy was different, at least that's what Grandma Gurley always used to tell her.' Jessica smiled, a lost smile submerged in the memory of her family. 'Mum didn't spend much time with him. He was gone when she was born, mixed up in the fighting in Palestine, gone again soon after he got back from the war.'

'Different I get,' said Harry. 'But what was that hostility I felt at the house, where I found this? It just about floored me!' The book perched precariously in his hand, at arms-length, drifting left and right until Jessica lurched forward from the couch, enfolding the volume in protective hands.

'Don't know,' she said. 'Maybe we'd better start reading it properly to find out?'

Harry remembered his reaction in the ruined house. The resentment all around him in the derelict room – it made him shudder. Was it all just his overactive imagination, a consequence of the weeks spent searching for even the slightest hint of Jimmy, scraps of information that might lead to something, anything beyond the weariness he felt?

The bitterness in the house had grown: when he ran, it threatened to crush him beneath rapidly stirring raw anger, the violence of it making him shudder once again. Harry wondered if Jessica acknowledged or even vaguely understood what he described.

'I just couldn't stay there any longer,' he said. 'Something drew me to that end of the room, then seemed to kick me in the guts trying to make me back off.'

'Who ...' Jessica reached out, laying a hand softly on Harry's shoulder. 'Who? What do you think it was?'

Harry, eyes to the floor, took a deep breath. 'Well, the first thing that comes to mind is Jimmy.' He looked up, expecting Jessica's doubt, perhaps ridicule.

Jessica shook her head. 'Everything I know about my grandfather says he wasn't an angry man.'

'Then who, or what?' said Harry, relieved at the absence of derision.

'I don't know,' she said. 'But maybe, as I said, the answer is in this diary. Jimmy left Grandma Gurley, Uncle Cara and mum, because he said Eiric needed him, that they had done things in

Palestine that only they could understand. Gurley said she could see the change in him. A sort of dread.'

'Dread, of what?'

'No, not dread exactly,' she said. 'Loss ... loss of everything that mattered to him, of all the important things he valued before he went away to that war. And they were related, half-brothers.'

Harry sat silently for a moment. Half-brothers didn't really explain the abandonment of Gurley, his children, his embrace of nomadic life.

'Maybe you're right. We'll find the answer in his journal,' he said finally, without the conviction he should have displayed.

Jessica's fingers moved across the volume as if trying to retrieve, through her fingertips, the essence of the story. She lowered her eyes to the floor. If Harry hadn't known better, he would have thought she was praying, seeking guidance from some divine entity, searching amongst the myriad of gods, beseeching the spirits for a way. *Well*, he thought, *we need all the help we can get to work this out, even from those mythical beings, so no harm in laying an each-way bet.*

*

August 31
Late evening

As Harry gently massaged his damaged fingers, Jessica raised her hands, palms to the ceiling. 'I feel something, vague like it's trying to hide, ducking for cover.' The book rested benignly in her left hand. 'Do you feel it?'

Harry closed his eyes, trying to project his senses towards

Jessica and the book. 'No,' he said. Nothing …' He let the statement hang for a moment. 'Maybe I'm just not able to tune in to things like this?'

'No,' Jessica said. 'You felt the strong mood in the ruin. This is very weak, as if it wants to be found but is afraid of something, it's backing away from discovery.'

'That could be why I was drawn to the spot in the first place. Then it changed its mind.'

'Or something changed its mind for it?' Jessica's fingers closed protectively about the volume.

Harry recalled again the malevolence that had suddenly replaced his compulsion to probe the rubble. He preferred to believe that his overactive imagination and fatigue had driven his flight, that there was no evil at work, just an old book containing the memories of a man who had been to war and not recovered from the experience. He absently bit into his bottom lip.

Jessica shook her head. 'You're not sure, are you Harry?'

Harry looked up into Jessica's intense gaze. 'No.'

'Well, no use debating it,' she said, finality in her voice. 'Let's get reading. Hopefully, find out how and why Jimmy did what he did.'

'We mightn't like what we find,' he said. 'Jimmy abandoned everything. Why and for what? And we still don't know what actually happened to him, personally, I mean, where's his body?'

Harry fell silent, a thought suddenly striking him. 'I mean, could he be actually buried under all that rubble at the ruin?'

'Who knows, Harry.' Jessica's voice filled with frustration. 'Enough stalling. We need to read!'

Harry suddenly didn't want any part of this, and he realised Jessica saw it in his face. Perhaps she saw other things too, like a lifetime of running away, shirking responsibility for his actions, the hurt his selfishness had inflicted on others, all in his eyes as he fought the urge to look away.

'We've come too far, Harry.' Jessica's hands moved in unison with the words. 'The feeling at the ruin. Forget that feeling. Your past disappointments are behind you. No one here cares about them. You don't need to run anymore. It's a choice. Either be a part of something good or piss off and be a miserable failure, again.'

She'd picked him. She knew he'd rise against the prospect of repeated failure, a return to the dysfunction of the past, the self-loathing that came from the very wellspring that they now sought. She knew him for what he was.

Harry baulked at being so easily read. He looked at Jessica, trying to calm his inner fears, his inner demons. He had sought the obscurity of drifting pastimes, of the beach house, abandonment of responsibility for others. Perhaps, like Jimmy, these diversions were doomed to fail.

'We've found what we came for. You can read the journal; take your time,' Harry said. 'We can talk about what you've found …' His voice faded. He looked at Jessica. She looked away towards the door. 'I'm just a phone call away. It will be easy.'

Jessica was silent. Harry had backed away from the brink, away from loyalty, turning the clock back, sliding back into his pathetic avoidance where commitment bound others but not him.

'Thanks, Harry,' Jessica said. Her lips were thin, the words almost snarled. 'You've every right to pull the pin on all this. After all, Jimmy wasn't your direct family, just the illegitimate son of your great-grandfather. And a blackfella to boot! I'll run you to the train station.'

Harry sat still. They looked at each other in crackling silence. Jessica's eyes reminded Harry of the twilight alpine sky as it deepened from complex indigos to the infinite hues of the fathomless night. He couldn't do it, not when there was hope.

'We've managed to survive this far, Jessica. But where's this taking us?' Harry said, pointing to the journal. 'I've got a feeling there's heartache and more in there.'

*

Reclining heavily against the back of the motel couch, Harry pulled himself from the memory of those first days of the search. The motel room felt suddenly suffocating, heat rising in his body, flushing his face. *What had he got himself into?*

Jessica stood motionless for a moment, her delicate mouth compressed into a thin line, finally shrugging, a slight elevation of her shoulders when she felt frustrated with the response of others. She moved quickly to the couch, dropped roughly, close to Harry, rested the book gently in her lap and turned to the first page. 'Let's read,' she said. 'Now!'

In his mind, Harry groaned and recalled fruitlessness of the search so far, the waning of the excitement that had led them from the coast into the mountains and back again, the great circle that everything seemed to form. He just didn't want to be caught in a whirlpool, in the hurricanes' vortex, the spiral of emotion that could reduce you to despair.

CHAPTER 12

September 1
Early morning

When Jessica stood, Harry glanced at his watch. It took him a while to realise that so much time had passed.

'It's three,' he said.

Jessica bent backwards, hands clasped on her hips, stretching with eyes closed. 'Harry,' she said. 'We've only just started.'

Harry shook his head. 'Let's take a break. In the morning, we'll have clearer heads, better memory for all this.' He pointed a finger at the journal that lay in his lap.

Jessica looked reluctantly at him, finally nodding her head.

'This journal is all over the place,' Harry said. 'I need to get my thoughts together to work out the timing of all the bits and pieces.'

Jessica nodded again and yawned, heading for the bedroom door. 'Okay, see you in the morning, Harry. Breakfast at nine, at the café down the road.' The last of the words were muffled by the closing door.

The light dimmed, Harry stretched out on the couch, adjusting several of the randomly scattered cushions beneath his head. A former life would have meant him seeking to share the bed with Jessica, but now, he didn't mind being relegated to the settee, despite the lack of comfort. He thought of Anika, wondering where she lay this night, whether the resolve she had shown before she left for Bangladesh still remained; if her promise to return to him, to make a life with him, was still her desire. The scrawled journal text moved through his mind: the loops, the sweeps of the handwriting, the distress, all the grief that was enshrouded in words and images. Jimmy seemed almost despairing of the mess that his life had become. Harry recognised the parallel with those men who had gravitated to the construction of the Snowy Scheme in the fifties – rejected, displaced, rootless men in search of purpose and meaning after the horror and destruction of war.

Harry recalled the journal's first pages, the opening passages:

Horse comes to me, in my dreams, sometimes in the middle of the day. He just appears. He doesn't accuse me of desertion, that I abandoned him, or murder, though God knows he has the right. It's like he is trying to get me to tell others what happened, why it happened, why we got ourselves into that mess, the dreadful things we had to do. He doesn't blame me, but he's pissed off at the way I let go of Gurley, Cara and Gima, the way I let Eiric destroy everything the way he did, including himself.

But I just can't do it. I can't look them all in the face and admit to the things we did, the thing I did.

Harry didn't know who or what the horse was. Jessica couldn't explain; didn't understand the things that seemed to torment Jimmy – the mess, the dreadful things? What desertion, what abandonment, other than his notable leaving of Gurley and family? The emotion in the text puzzled Harry; everything he knew about Jimmy indicated a person with both feet firmly planted on the ground, a reasoning, composed man, not given to whimsy.

Harry drifted into light sleep, images flowing, hovering through his mind, until ...

A sharp push at his shoulder!

Harry shoved it away.

Another, rough this time!

'Harry!'

He just wanted it to go away!

'Harry!' More insistent this time.

Eyes open, confused, Harry stared into Jessica's face.

'Harry, wake up!'

'What?'

'You're shouting.'

'What?' Harry shook his head, heaved himself upright, swinging his legs free of the loose, tangled blanket, bare feet on the lino floor, distress in his face.

Jessica abruptly stepped back. 'You were dreaming,' she said. 'What's happened?'

'Something about the Negev,' said Harry, shaking his head again, eyes lowered, hands clasped at his temples. 'I was there ... I was there. I saw it happen.'

'What? Where? What happened?' A look of deep concern clouded Jessica's face.

Harry took a deep, shuddering breath. 'I've got to think,' he said. 'I've got to catch this before it fades.'

Jessica started to talk. 'I don't understand ...'

Harry waved a hand. 'Quiet! I've got to concentrate!'

Silence.

Jessica slowly lowered herself into the opposing chair, the creak of the timber frame the only sound. Her eyes focused on Harry as if searching for his next words.

The silence stretched into minutes.

'I don't know what this means, but ...' he said finally, interrupted by a deep breath, this time to calm himself. 'He had a gun, a revolver, you know, one of those old-fashioned ones with a spinning wheel, like the cowboys have. He just walked up to the soldier, pressed the barrel to his head and blew his head to pieces.'

'Who?' said Jessica. 'Who did this?'

'Not sure. But it could have been Jimmy. Who else could it be.'

'Right, well maybe it's just your imagination working overtime after what we read in the journal?'

'Yeah, maybe.' Harry wasn't convinced. 'But, it was so real!'

'Dreams can be like that.'

'That's not all,' Harry said, looking up at Jessica. 'There was a horse.'

'Yes, Jimmy mentioned horses in his writing.'

'No, not just any horse.' Harry held Jessica's eyes. 'This was Horse, the name Jimmy gave to his horse, his friend, the other friend who went with him to Palestine.'

Hesitation.

'Yes, go on.' Jessica was anxious to get on with this.

'A big horse, intelligent eyes, confident, who could talk without moving its mouth.'

Jessica nodded her head. 'You're just overtired, Harry. It's your brain clearing away the junk from today, jumbling Jimmy's writing into random images.'

Harry used the tips of his fingers to massage his temples. 'Maybe you're right,' he said. 'Maybe we need to get some uninterrupted sleep before we tackle Jimmy's book again ...Yeah, but I don't want more of this.' Harry felt distressed by the vivid images that now haunted him.

Jessica leant close to Harry, resting a soft hand on his shoulder. 'Try and get a couple more hours sleep. It's almost five. It'll be light soon.' She rose, walked to the bedroom door, stopped and turned to face Harry as he subsided onto the couch.

'Harry, you said the horse spoke.' A pensive look. 'What did it say?'

A moment to recall. 'The horse said that time doesn't heal; rather, we can only heal ourselves by understanding what those before us have been through.'

Jessica stood at the door, silent for a moment, finally turning and disappearing through the dark portal. Harry once again heard a muffled, 'Goodnight, Harry', as the door gently closed.

Harry lay again in a darkened room, unable to submit to sleep, mind churning through vague images, through the cryptic conversations within the dream. He suddenly remembered the horse's other words; he sat upright, wondering if their quest, their examination of Jimmy's journal would bring release or regret to their lives:

He killed in the name of loyalty, friendship, and compassion, yet it seemed it was without sympathy for the impact of his actions on those he left behind.

CHAPTER 13

September 1
Midday

Jessica didn't seem to want to talk. She looked away from Harry to the waiter as he hurried between tables, sweeping through the crowded patrons with plates held aloft. Her mouth was set in a thin line, reminding Harry of a former lover, someone who could turn from engaging smile to critical exactitude, even rampant savagery, in an instant.

'The journal,' said Harry. 'It might not be Jimmy's writing.'

Jessica swivelled her eyes to Harry. 'There's too many familiar references, Harry.'

'Someone who might have met Jimmy, pinched his ideas, his persona? And anyway, what's someone like your grandfather doing writing a journal anyway?' Harry pushed his fingers through his hair, a contemplative gesture, one that seemed to irritate Jessica.

She blinked. 'Harry, you're trying too hard to be negative. Things referred to in the book, only Jimmy and Grandma Gurley would have known. He was an unusual man for the times. His feet were planted in the whitefella as well as the blackfella camps. It has to be him.'

Harry transferred his attention to the distance, from the balcony overlooking the bay that swept north, to the river-mouth. They were sitting at a table beneath the warm autumn sun, with half-eaten food and partly consumed wine. Harry didn't want the dulling effect of food and alcohol.

'The last of my school days were spent in this pub,' he said.

'Nothing much has changed is my guess,' Jessica said, a look of mild reproof.

'Lots.' Harry gazed absently into the distance. 'I mean, it's changed a lot. This place was virtually a dump then, ready to be condemned.'

'Looks like it now.' Jessica unimpressed.

'We didn't care, then. The beer was cheap, it was open on Sundays, and I had enough money working at the brickworks; enough to get pissed.'

'Misspent youth.' Jessica laughed.

'It's heritage-listed now,' Harry said. He looked up at the freshly-painted timber structure. 'Along with the wharf down the road.'

'The coasters used to collect farming produce from the valley. It took over a week to travel down from Sydney by road. The Illawarra Steamship Company. They brought in the miners during the gold rush at Kiandra. It was a hard walk into the mountains from here, to the Monaro through the top of the valley.' Jessica knew more of the area's history than Harry – he felt like a latter-day interloper.

'We used to have a few beers,' he said. 'While waiting for the big swell to arrive. Then, if it wasn't too dark, we'd go down to the wharf, jump in from there and paddle to the back of the break.'

'Like I said, misspent youth.'

Harry thought for a moment, the glare from the day making him squint at the distant shore. Misspent was probably only part of it, for his youth had been devoted to reinforcing the fault lines in his character, setting himself up for relationship dysfunction and self-loathing. He had been oblivious of the influence of the past. The war had done so much damage: the disintegration of his family, the ceaseless authority of past suffering. He was now borne on the current of Jessica's drive to unravel those influences, to define the foundations of her own inhibitions. It was hard, he thought, to understand the impact of past events, hard to tease apart the stream of trials, to differentiate cause from effect.

'I knew I had to get away from here,' he said as he drew a deep breath. 'But I didn't know what to do when I did. I failed for a time in my studies and for years couldn't decide on a career. I blundered through my affairs, each one slowly disintegrating, generally without rancour, just fading away.' He paused, looking to the horizon once again. 'I didn't recognise my own failure, didn't have any understanding of closure, how to get it, or even what it was.'

Jessica remained silent, her absorbing, dark, fathomless gaze resting on Harry, tense, as if on the brink of a nervous rebuttal. She opened her mouth as if to talk, then relaxed her face, nodding her head. Harry reckoned Jessica knew she was being used, that this search was a means to his ends, as a way of finding a solution to his own defects. She didn't seem to mind. No doubt he was being used as well, a catalyst in the search for answers to the confusion that encircled her family, her life.

Harry shrugged his shoulders. What did it matter, people using people, as long as it led to something positive, and no one was hurt? Guilt suddenly stabbed at him, the wreckage that was his life dancing before him – Frances, the baby, Teresa, all sacrificed on the altar of his dysfunction, Anika now absorbed in the rescue of South Asia, lost to him, perhaps, never to be found?

What had Anika said before leaving? Harry closed his eyes, enthralled by the memory of Anika's delicate features, her long, bare legs pressed against him, her rhythmic motion capturing his mind, his soul, consuming the summit of his passion. *The past lives in us*, she said, *the good things and the bad. If we're going to have any chance at resolution, we need to dig into those past lives, see what happened, try to understand.*

The distant sound of waves against the rocks and the sandy beach down the hill pulled him from his reverie. He felt an overwhelming desire to pick up the phone, call Anika, explain his dilemma.

'Well, talking of getting away,' Jessica said with laughter, a deep, resonant, excited laugh. 'We came back here, to the coast, because we needed somewhere quiet to go through the journal. So, let's get after it.'

Harry shook off his need, jerked back to reality by a singular, driven mind; she had deflected his neediness, his gloomy admissions. He stood, pushing back the chair, the clatter against the timber deck turning the heads of nearby patrons. 'Right.' He smiled as he walked away. 'My turn to pay, I think.'

Payment would indeed be swift. He would soon be immersed in the past as they delved into the scratchy writing, the confusing reflections, the disjointed timeline of Jimmy's reminiscences.

As he walked to the cashier, an image of Anika again filled his mind, tall, elegant, composed, resolute, the strains of her mellifluous voice, her ability to appreciate the influences of past generations on her life. A deep longing flashed through him. When would he see her again?

*

Harry stopped turning the page, his eyes focusing on the words – a statement that carried a sense of sorrow:

The land carried us from high country towards the coast. Ed, Ngarigo people elder, leading, has the way, knows the country, can feel the way. Horse would know country as well if he was here, and even in Palestine where them bastards made me do things I can't forget. But he's gone, still in my mind though, talking to me, telling me to go home. But I can't go, don't know the way, too much bad stuff kicking around. Ed singing the way. Never learned the songs, never initiated, not my country. Another week, then the coast.

Harry lifted his eyes from the book, focusing on Jessica as she sat quietly on the lounge opposite, reading from her book copy.

'Jimmy came to the coast from the mountains ...'

Jessica raised her eyes to meet Harry. 'Yes, they had their trails. Summer in the mountains, cool, winter on the coast.'

'But why?' said Harry. 'He wasn't a mountain local. His people, the Kamilaroi, were to the north in the New England and out on the plains towards Walgett.'

Jessica shook her head. 'Don't know. But what I do know ...' She quickly turned a few of the pages. '... is that he saw some horrible things in Palestine. Listen to this – she read:

Bodies, piles of them, crammed into the gorge. Could take the fighting, reckon the hand-to-hand was just them or me, but machine gunning them down like that. No. Burying them all afterwards, the stink, shit and blood. Can't forget it all.

'And this.' Jessica glanced up, eyes close to tears.

Waking up all the time. Can't sleep. Lots of memories crowding in my head. Gurley, the kids. Where are they now? Horse. Couldn't bring his spirit home. Them bastards wouldn't let him come. Should have just taken off. We would have found a way home. Buralga. Where's he now, poor bugger lost everything.

Harry carefully placed his copy of the journal to the side on the couch, stood, moving to the window that overlooked the banksia forest, the beach and ocean in the distance. For a moment, he stood quietly, the only noise the faint whisper of the sea breeze and the muffled swoosh of the waves. 'These names,' he said. 'Who or what are they?'

'Does it matter?' Jessica was emphatic. 'It's Jimmy's story we're after.'

Silence.

'Yeah,' Harry said. 'Yeah, it does. We need to establish the network, the web of associations that surrounded Jimmy. The people, the ones that mattered to him, the ones he either abandoned or held on to. We need to know what mattered to him, mattered enough to write it down.'

'But that could take forever.'

'Jessica,' Harry ran fingers through his hair, frustrated. 'You told me this was important, this sifting through Jimmy's thoughts.' He moved back to the couch, leant forward to emphasise his words, his irritation breaking free in the movement of his hands. 'I would have left it to you, but you want me here as support? Another viewpoint? A means of picking up what you might miss? I don't know ...'

Harry dropped his hands into his lap, relaxed his tense back against the seat. 'I don't really know what your motivations for all this are, but what I do know now is that unless we uncover the web, this network of relationships, like my grandfather's relationship with Jimmy and why Jimmy disappeared the way he did, I'm not going to understand myself, and why my life is such a bloody mess!'

Jessica nodded, silent.

'And my guess is, neither are you.'

'My life's not a mess.' Jessica was defiant.

'No, granted, not like mine.' Harry repentant. 'But you need answers, just like I do.'

Silence enveloped them. Harry regretted his words, harsh, accusative, complaining. He felt he stood at a crossroads: one-way led to possible enlightenment, just a chance, the other to more of the same dull, grey abandonment of happiness, acceptance of lonely misery, separation from any possibility of feeling. An image of Anika once again flooded through him, her words, her confidence, her stability. She had delved deeply into her family's past and emerged as a different person, not cured of that history, instead at peace with her place in the continuum, accepting of its influence, ready to repudiate its hold.

'Yeah, you're right, Harry. Probably more so.'

'Why?' Harry needed Jessica's grounding.

'Because my family, my people have been crushed by invasion and discrimination for so long.'

'Everyone has that in their past. The first of my family in Australia landed as prisoners of the British at Sydney Cove.'

'Yes, right. But you are whitefellas. As the generations passed, the bad things were forgotten, your ancestry even becoming a badge of honour. We haven't had that luxury.'

What could Harry say? She was right. He had no right to complain about his lot, and yet ...

'Jessica, there's something else working here, something chipping away at us, at our souls. Something happened to Jimmy, to my grandfather, something that still lives in us.'

'Mum warned me that there were things in Jimmy's past that wouldn't be easy to accept. He didn't even talk to Grandma Gurley about the time he spent in Palestine, certainly not mum.'

'Well, if we stop talking, read his words, find people he knew if we can, we might be able to piece it together?'

Jessica sat, her eyes glazed, lost in thought, silent so long that

Harry considered getting up to leave: perhaps an afternoon surf would clear his head, renew his desire to press ahead with this seemingly fruitless search.

He stood.

'I need to go home for a while,' Jessica said.

'What?' Harry stopped his walk to the stairs and the freedom of the ocean.

'I need to talk to mum.'

'You can do that on the phone.'

'Mum hates phones. She's old fashioned. Can't manage these smartphones.'

'Why?' He seemed to be asking *why* rather a lot – like in his childhood, the standard answer was: *Because y is a crooked letter and doesn't know better.* He laughed to himself.

'Harry, she's old, and I need to get into her memories. Anything that Grandma Gurley might have said about some of the things in Jimmy's journal.'

'Like who's Horse and Buralga?'

'Yeah, she might know, might remember, but I've got to do it face-to-face. Otherwise, she'll just get confused.'

Harry continued to the stairs, to the shed and his surfboard, and the only freedom he knew, the release of the ocean's waves. 'Take the car,' he said as he clattered down to stairs. 'See you when you get back.'

*

The ocean was a release, the paddle out to the break, the rip along the rocks that carried him, with minimum effort, washing away his doubts. It was a liberation from earthly matters. There was always a reset, the mind focusing on one thing – the take-off on a wave. If you got that right, the rest would automatically follow; the turn parallel to the wave, the drop to the bottom, the subtle shift in weight, the surfboard's response. He paddled hard, felt the slight lift of the board's nose against the offshore breeze, shifting his weight to counteract the wind as it started to blow hard against him. The wave seemed to pause. He dug deeper with his arms, hands pushing against a whole ocean of water, felt a sudden surge behind, a boot up the bum that hurled him onto the cresting wave, onto the gleaming face that now formed a treacherous cliff. He was standing, feeling the power, watching for the tell-tale collapse of the wall ahead, a dissolution that would indicate he had picked the wrong wave. The precipice stayed intact. He raced forward, his flight filling him with joy, ecstasy that removed him from the despondency of the search, separating him from the choices that had led him into dark places.

One, two, three turns. One more, and he would exhaust the wave's power.

A mountain of water descended on his head, the world a mess of white foaming bubbles – a tonne of ocean holding him down, dragging him to the bottom in the surge, turning him.

Which way was up?

Breath running thin now!

Arms flailing, searching for daylight, flighting for breath, his lungs about to collapse, resisting the urge to breathe in the salty, aqueous mix. Into the froth, hands without solid purchase, no buoyancy here, legs kicking nothing. So, this was what the end was like – a whimper, not a shout.

Light!

Push!

Air!

Harry desperately dragged air into his lungs, cold water sluicing down his throat – another breaking wave arriving to seek his demise. He struggled against the tide.

Another wave!

He was too old for this battle, fighting the ocean, resisting life's flood, the force of time, the might of the past. Harry would ring Anika, tell her he was giving up, that he was returning to the path that he understood, accepting that he would be ignorant of the influences of the past. A new life would be forged. He didn't need to understand, didn't need to dig into the travails of those poor sods who had been destroyed by war and bigotry. He had the love of a beautiful woman – what more did he need?

Harry felt a tug on his ankle – the tethered surfboard demanding attention – he pulled the leg rope, the board skidding to him, obedient, compliant, eager. More waves?

He paddled to the beach, stood for a moment, silently watching the succession of cresting waves as they peeled around the point, their foaming crests luminous in the sun as it sank towards evening. At last, he turned, to labour through the heavy, soft sand to the car park and the track through the banksia forest, to his home, his sanctuary, his fortress.

Chapter 14

September 3

Harry was dozing on the veranda, on the dilapidated daybed, the bed he had rescued from Ricko's place all those years ago. He had often wondered what unnatural acts had been performed on the bed, the thought becoming an obsession until he'd carted the mattress to the tip and bought a new one, clean and devoid of any questionable carnal history.

He lay in half-sleep, dreaming a vision of Anika, her arrival, their reunion, a connection he so desired when she called. He fought to rise through the layers of slumber, clinging to the comfortable blanket of sleep, hoping the birds would abandon their raucous call. Finally, he gave up, let the noise wake him, squinting against the bright day, grabbing the phone.

'Yeah.'

'It's Jes.' Jessica, a distant, reedy voice down a tube from somewhere.

'Oh, hi Jessica.' Harry swung his legs across the bed, lowering them to the deck, a faint breeze blowing upward through the boards.

'I'm on my way south,' she said. 'I'll be there just after lunch.'

'Where are you now?'

'South of Wollongong.'

'How'd it go with your mum?'

'She wants to see them.'

'See what?'

'Everything.'

'Might be a bit hard for an old lady.'

'Yeah, I know. But she's a tough old bird. She's insistent and reckons she'll see more than we did.'

'Did she tell you anything? Any clues?'

'Lots. It'll help translate what's in the book. Tell you when I get there.'

Harry dropped the phone onto the bed, stood, heading for the bathroom. His mouth was dry, cheeks sticking to teeth. *Shouldn't sleep during the day*, he thought. *It always ends with this half-awake confusion and a mouth like the bottom of a parrot's cage.* The tension of the last week, though, had left him saturated with tiredness, a feeling that he could go no further, curiosity abandoned, a victim of the sunshine, and the irresistible comfort of the deck. He stared at bloodshot eyes, whites marbled with streaks of red. He'd have to repair the damage before Anika arrived, whenever that might be.

He returned to the deck, sitting heavily at the edge of the daybed, gazing absently at the banksia forest that crowded about the house. He was tempted to roll to the horizontal again, showed extreme fortitude, deciding instead to remain upright, gazing through the trees to the beach beyond and the crash of the surf, the waft of salt air, the lure of waves. *Too late*, he thought. *I shouldn't have slept. The afternoon onshore breeze will have stuffed the surf up by now.*

Faint music drifted to him on the growing sea breeze, a band playing at the pub on the headland, people eating, drinking, enjoying a lazy afternoon, watching the surf, the bay, the distant river mouth as the day and the brilliant sunshine gradually submitted to the planet's spin, more music and the appetites of the evening. He thought of Anika, their last broken conversation as she ran from the ravages of a storm; she who kept such a positive view of the world amidst the misery of the delta, the cyclones, monsoons, the floods, the sentence that antiquity could so easily apply.

A positive view. There was so much darkness in Anika's family, yet she had subjugated its impact.

A raucous bird call.

'Harry here.'

'Harry. Andy.'

'Andy, long time, no hear.' Harry's thoughts were swept away.

'Too long, mate.'

'What's up?'

'Well, we need you back in harness.'

Silence as Harry pondered a response.

'There are some issues with the West African divestment.'

'I thought that was under Teresa's control.'

'Was. But seems she's having second thoughts.'

'Second thoughts? About what?'

Hesitation.

'Everything.'

'Everything? Does that mean she's decided not to be human or something?' *Or maybe she suddenly wants to be human*, Harry thought.

'Seems she's fallen in love.'

'What?' Harry couldn't think of anyone Teresa loved more than herself.

'Yeah. Fallen in love. Wants to have babies and things.'

'Who the hell with?'

'Harry, brace yourself.'

'Yeah, I'm braced.'

'She says she's in love with you. Says you had an agreement that once the West African thing was set, you'd get together.'

Harry dredged through conversations, sifting through statements made before he left Africa – there was nothing, no commitment, no promise, just ...

A vague memory.

A passing comment made by Teresa, an assurance that they would reunite once the African business was done. At the time, Harry had seen it as a release, another convenient promise shrouded in ambition.

'I haven't spoken to Teresa for months, maybe more than six months,' said Harry. 'Not since I left Africa for Bangladesh.'

'Well, she's convinced,' Andy said, severity in the voice. 'Harry, you've got to sort this out.'

'Andy, this isn't my doing. She's gone bonkers. There's lots of water under the bridge since then.'

'No matter, Harry. You're the one she's focused on. You had an affair with her. You sort it out.'

'My mess, heh.' Harry felt disinclined to be the fall guy.

'Yep. She's making landfall in Sydney next week, Friday. Staying at the Hilton.'

The phone went dead. Andy wasn't asking or being polite – Harry was thrown back into reality, accountability, duty. He supposed it was time he accepted responsibility for his past actions. Until he did so, how could he honestly approach the future?

*

The waiter lumbered past a nest of patrons, a tray of spent food, plates held aloft, dodging past a sudden, expansive gesture from a member of the crowd. *It's a fine line*, Harry thought, *how success or failure relies so much on chance. The wrong path selected, a wayward choice amongst myriad options, everything hanging in the balance. What direction to take? No way of knowing at the time.*

The waiter swept past him, headed for the kitchen sanctuary, no doubt to be primed for a reprise, another foray into an accidental world. Harry lifted the glass, a pint, half consumed, observing the alcohol-fuelled revelry, the mix of holidaymakers and locals, male, female, mostly just post-adolescent, direct from the beach to the pub on the headland, anticipating a night's partying. A scantily-clad female careered through the door from the hotel's veranda, swayed past, no doubt on the way relieving the pressure of the carousing – so much liquid being absorbed – Harry noting the swell of her thinly-veiled breasts, the curve of her bare hips and buttocks. He set the glass back on the bar, immediately feeling like an old pervert, no longer acceptable in such company, no longer of any interest to such a gathering. He abandoned the remainder of the pint, heading for the door, strangely disgusted with himself, or was it sadness, sorrow at lost desirability, the evaporation of allure.

Harry squinted as he emerged from the noisy bar onto the pub veranda, into the glare of the mid-afternoon sun, almost blind as his eyes adjusted to the light. He grabbed for the rail beside the steps, steadying himself before plunging down to the road and his car parked nearby.

'Harry.' A voice from behind.

Harry turned; eyes still blind.

'Jes. How did you find me?'

'You weren't home. Your surfboard was. So, I reckoned you might be here.'

'Lucky, I was just leaving.'

'Going home?'

'Yeah. Had enough of all this.' He jerked his thumb at the crowd, excited voices, loud hilarity emphasising his point.

'You poor old bastard, Harry. Too old now for a session at the pub?'

Harry stood, resentment welling as his eyes regained vision. 'So, Jes. You've just arrived?' Harry wanted to divert talk away from any investigation of his attitude or age. *Perversion*, he thought, *came in many guises, but certainly one of them would have been any attempt by him to hit on one of those beach girls.*

'Yeah. And we need to talk. Mum had quite a few ideas about what we found.'

'Right. So, let's talk,' said Harry. 'At home. Did you walk up to the pub or drive?'

'Walked,' Jessica said. 'Looking for you on the way, on the beach.'

Harry waved his arm, pointing the way to the car, relieved that the pub and its reminder of advancing years would be consigned to a distant disturbance, the music and carousing a vague disorder drifting along the coast.

*

September 4

The Sydney hotel receptionist was neat, shiny dark hair pulled back, tied into a tidy knot, efficiency in every move. Harry smelt cleanliness in her soapy fragrance. Anika would have recoiled; perfume yes, a soapy fragrance, no.

'Mrs Worth is not answering,' she said. 'Would you like to leave a message?'

'No, I'll wait.' Harry walked to the foyer holding-pen, sat, wishing Andy had provided a phone number. The sooner this was over, the better.

And the sooner he returned to the beach house, the better would be their chances of solving the Jimmy enigma – his travels, whereabouts, his fate. It wasn't Jimmy's end that now interested Harry; instead, it was the manner of his living, the life events that shaped the path he took to its conclusion. Harry now saw how events could profoundly set not only one's own course but also the trajectory of others, sometimes generations apart. He sat, submerged in the muzak sterility, mind wandering to the last evening, the conversation with Jessica, at the beach house.

'Mum said the loss of Jimmy's horse was the key to Jimmy's disappearance,' said Jessica.

'The horse? Why was the horse so important?' Harry said.

'It was spiritual. Their connection was more than horse and rider, much more. He was called Horse.'

'That's original.' Harry instantly regretted his sarcasm, hastily adding: 'So why take such an important connection like that into danger, into a war zone?'

'Jimmy apparently was following Horse's wishes. Grandma Gurley said so. Said Horse wanted to stay close, to guard him, shield him against the worst things.'

'Treacherous ground, a war zone,' said Harry. 'And one so far from home. Chances were, none of them would make it home, horses or riders.'

'Horse went.' Jessica said. 'But he didn't make it home.'

A pause.

'And it wasn't a bullet in battle that stopped Horse. It was Jimmy.'

Another pause.

'And your grandfather, Jimmy's brother, lost a horse as well.'

'Grandad, Eiric, never mentioned it.' *Never really talked about the war*, he thought. *They all just seemed to fold the memories of it into themselves.*

'He loved his horses,' Harry said.

'Atonement.' Jessica rested easily against the back of Richo's daybed, her arms spread wide against the backrest.

'Atonement? For what?' A stupid question, too late to withdraw.

Jessica answered anyway. 'For leaving their mates behind.' She paused. 'Worse. For having to kill them rather than just abandon them, after they'd carried them through hell, and in the end won a stunning victory.'

'Hence, Jimmy's paintings in the cave.' But, how did a bunch of paintings help make amends?

Silence descended on the veranda, the distant party at the pub filtering through the crash of the surf. The swell was rising – tomorrow would be a good test of skill as the waves wrapped around the south point, past the old wharf.

'So, what else did your mum tell you?'

'That she wanted to see the paintings.'

Yes, and how could that be possible for a lame, old lady? 'Photos,' Harry said as if that would solve everything. Another self-evident solution.

'Jim's gone back with a camera, but he's insistent that no one else but us knows about the place.'

Harry nodded, wondering how long they could keep such a place secret, whether it was right to do so, certainly in the long run.

'We've still got the book.' Harry said it as if that was some consolation. 'Did your Mum unravel any of that riddle?'

Jessica stood, walking slowly along the veranda, finally turning slowly to face Harry. 'Some things, though, she said, most of it was beyond her memory. Couldn't remember much, only thin memories of Gurley talking about the war.'

'Too bad,' Harry said. 'Most of it's gibberish to me.'

'Except …' Jessica let the word merge with the distant thunder of the waves on the shore.

'Except, what?'

'Burralga.'

'Yeah, I remember the word. Jimmy wrote it lots.'

'And Yaama dhagaan.'

Harry nodded. He remembered the text, the spidery writing, no doubt penned by a campfire somewhere, perhaps even in the caves. 'They usually went together.'

'Yeah, Mum remembers Grandma Gurley talking about Burralga.'

'Well, that's something. It means …?' Harry was tired of the mystery.

'Harry, it's a name. The name Jimmy gave to your grandfather.'

Harry was silent for a moment, the faint sea breeze strengthening now, carrying away the stickiness of a still, sultry evening, salty moisture he could almost taste.

'It means?' Harry wanted an answer.

'Brolga. It means brolga, Harry, in Kamilaroi.' Jessica laughed a soft chuckle. 'Mum said it was Jimmy's bit of fun about your grandfather's nose; big like a bird's beak.'

Harry nodded.

'Perhaps I should call you that too.' A devilish gleam in Jessica's eyes. 'Your nose is rather prominent as well.'

'Maybe you should.' Harry could feel the turn of the wheel, the turn of the cycle from those distant generations, a rotation that fed the uncertainty he felt so profoundly. 'And the other words?'

'Hello, brother.'

Harry, thought about the significance of the words. Finally, he said, 'He knew!' And it explained so much: his closeness to Eiric and his brothers, his journey into the jaws of death when he could easily have avoided the conflict, his loyalty to Eiric, even after the war when things went so wrong.

He suddenly felt a presence, looking up from his reverie on the hotel lounge.

'Hi, Harry.'

'Teresa.'

'Have you been waiting long?'

A quick glance at his watch as he rose from his seat. 'Not long. Is there somewhere private we can talk?'

'Yes, how about my room?'

'No,' he said, a little more severely than intended. 'I think we need more neutral ground.'

CHAPTER 15

INVITATION

September 4

In the street, tension driving him forward, his stride lengthened. Harry didn't hear the rumble and blare of the traffic. Teresa walked beside him, a silent lure, the distraction he feared, meddling with his faith in change, his belief that things had turned for the better, that he had found, no, created, a new path, a constructive view of his part in it all.

It was undeniable that Teresa had allure: intelligent, sensual, inventive. She had lost none of those captivating qualities. It took just a few words to rekindle yearning, craving that had always subjugated his being, that had repeatedly brought him to heal, drinking once more from the source.

'In here,' he said, abruptly turning right, through a heavy glass door, into the relative quiet of a small restaurant/bar, the traffic hubbub replaced with a background of music, the clink of glass and the murmur of a subdued crowd.

A waiter ushered them to a table. Drink orders taken, Harry was finally faced with the inevitable: a conversation with his nemesis.

'Off the hard stuff, Harry?' Teresa delivered the opening gambit, a wry smile, perhaps a smirk.

Harry gathered himself. 'What are you doing here, Teresa?' Nothing like the direct approach.

'Doing here?' Teresa returned a puzzled look. 'Harry, Sydney is the head office. I'm reporting in after a successful divestment.'

'Not what Andy said.' Harry struggled to neutralise sourness, to banish any cynicism in his voice.

'Andy's got problems.' Teresa offhand, brushing aside the comment.

'Problems?' Harry sceptical. 'The way he told it, the West African thing is staggering, teetering on failure.'

A laugh. Teresa's short, staccato snigger, hammering at Harry's ears. 'His problem is the board. He can't justify pulling me out of Africa, right when we're about to use the divestment proceeds to pile into some really great things further south.'

'So, you're the one to make it happen?'

Teresa hesitated. Harry could see the distraction of choice. 'Yes. The next twelve months are critical, but ...'

Here it comes, thought Harry. 'But?'

'Harry. You and me. It's time we took the leap.'

'What do you mean, take the leap?'

'When you left for Dhaka, you agreed we'd get together when the West Africa divestment was done.'

Harry's turn to hesitate, as he delved through the memory, finally saying, 'Selective memory there, Teresa. I believe that was your suggestion, not mine.'

'Never mind that,' she said. 'It was what we agreed.'

Teresa had been focused, the same focus Harry saw in her now. He saw her only briefly in those last days in Africa, sidelined by her devotion to career, her conviction that her trajectory was up, her path was to stardom, that Harry was "in the bag", safely tucked away for later consumption; so sure of her position, she had neglected subsequent contact. Now, Harry was faced with the same certainty: her conviction of his capitulation to her will – he would follow her strength as he always had. He saw her resolve, felt the determination and faltered under the weight, his vision blurring. It would be easy to climb aboard the Teresa train, go wherever it pleased her, no more concern, no more decisions, until …

Harry shook his head to clear his eyes.

Until …

Until Teresa found a new challenge, a more profitable path without Harry, perhaps with someone else?

'Harry,' Teresa was on the front foot. 'I've only got a few months, perhaps less, before the board will want me back to look after those new opportunities. I can do most of the early stuff from here. That buys me at least nine months without international travel, time enough to start a family, get that ball rolling.'

'What?' Harry felt himself recoil.

'Make a baby, you dunderhead.'

'What?' Harry felt the burden of an incoherent response.

'Am I not making myself clear?'

'Patently clear, Teresa.'

'Well then, we need to get started, no time to lose.' She started to rise from the chair. Harry resisted the reflex urge to follow.

'Ah, Teresa. You've got it all worked out, but ...' Harry was glued to the chair.

'What!' Irritation at Harry's rebuttal.

'There's a snag in your plan.' Harry took a deep breath, lifting his gaze to the rampant woman. 'Well, several actually, no, lots.'

*

'But why?' There was an ominous sound in Teresa's voice, the sort of growl that Harry remembered as a prelude to the shredding of an adversary or a hapless underling.

'It's not right.' Harry had to be careful. He knew how vindictive Teresa could be, had witnessed her inexorable pursuit of the unlucky few.

'What do you mean, *not right*?' Teresa wouldn't lose gracefully.

'Teresa, I have a child already, here in Sydney. That didn't go well. Bringing more children into the world would be irresponsible.'

'But, Harry, this is different.'

'Children are children. How is it different?'

Teresa was silent for a moment. Harry could see her gathering herself for a final assault, an attack designed he was sure to cripple his defences, outflank the trenches he'd hastily dug, his Maginot Line with all its inherent weaknesses.

Harry heard the deliberate, slow, measured intake of breath, saw the eyes move, fixed now on him, holding him within a fine net.

Oh, shit!

Were there tears?

Harry recognised the trap. Too late to run? Too late for a diversionary manoeuvre?

Unless ...

Unless he took the bull by the horns, revealed his feelings, told the truth, risked everything in an ultimate declaration.

Harry held Teresa's eyes. He recognised the ploy, the trick to degrade any response he might give, a manoeuvre derived from familiarity, brutal analysis of his character, dissection of his weaknesses into manageable, malleable pieces. Teresa's skill was admirable. Manipulation of circumstances was instinctive to her, yet he felt the wavering of his resolve for all his insight. Here was a beautiful woman who wanted a life with him, a family, the full catastrophe.

'I've wanted this for so long,' she said, tears welling in her eyes. She pulled a serviette from the table, dabbing it at her cheeks.

'There's someone else!' He blurted it out in haste, no subtle design.

Silence.

Harry waited for the change, the acid invective that would inevitably surface when Teresa was thwarted.

'Someone else?' Teresa said, her voice unnervingly soft. 'What does that mean?'

Harry didn't want to go into details. In his mind, he weighed the wisdom of even mentioning someone else, immediately rejecting the revelation of a name – a name would encourage unwelcome focus, maybe even retribution.

'It means, Teresa,' Harry drew in a deep breath, 'that there's someone else permanently in my life.'

Teresa's face hardened. 'Who is this bint?'

Harry fired back, 'It doesn't matter who, Teresa. The point is, I've moved on.' There, it was said, couldn't be retrieved. Harry sat amidst the bemused silence.

'Give me a name, Harry. Who is she?'

Harry stood his ground, at last feeling the encouragement of a backbone.

'I don't believe you. You're scared of a commitment, of the responsibility that a solid relationship and children would bring.' Teresa's mouth was a grim line.

Harry had to refute that notion. 'Children aren't the problem, Teresa.'

Teresa was now on the attack, cutting across Harry's words. 'Then let's give *us* a chance, at least see where it leads. We'll regret passing up this chance. One day you'll kick yourself if we don't. I'll even move in with you. Being domestic could be real fun.'

Harry felt disembodied, sensed his mind drifting from his body, could see himself from above, sitting opposite this resolute person, the steamroller of her intellect crushing the life from his feeble body. The future would be no different from the present – he would submit to the force of her will and be blown wherever the winds of her desires dictated, a tyrant demanding obedience, until ...

Until he was swept away as redundant, surplus to needs: out with the old, in with the new.

Silence again, except for the muffled murmur of the restaurant crowd and an occasional distant laugh. Harry couldn't see the joke. He had to extricate himself from this web, this place, this problem, his creation, a dilemma of his own making.

'No!' Harry needed to be careful, had to minimise the ire. 'For a start, Andy wants me in North Africa, starting next month.' Teresa leant forward, about to interject. Harry charged on. 'And that means I'll be away from here indefinitely.' It was a lie, the "being away" bit, but Harry felt it was believable.

'Secondly, right now, I'm fully occupied with a friend in searching for her grandfather.' Again, Teresa opened her mouth, ready to interject. Harry cut her off – his backbone was strengthening. 'And I cannot abandon her. She needs me in the search.'

'So, is that the one, your latest infatuation?'

Harry momentarily toyed with deception – he could say yes, a deflection of suspicion from Anika.

'No, she's a relative. We've been searching together. It's been an emotional journey.'

'Fine,' said Teresa, brushing away Harry's defence. 'But I don't see why we can't get together.'

'And thirdly,' Harry continued. 'I'm committed to someone for the first time in my life, and I can honestly say that. It's a belief in a positive future together.'

Harry suddenly felt solidity in his life, a strange sensation given the shifting sands of his existence, the insecurity of relationships like the one before him now. He just hoped that Anika was safe and had the same belief.

CHAPTER 16

RESPONSIBILITIES

September 5

Harry felt the weight, the burden of so many hours devoted to career, the constant demand for results, the manoeuvrings, the dismissal of authentic friendship: chess pieces sliding across a board. Andy, though, was different. They had a relationship, a bond that had persisted since their early days, those days at school. An unlikely alliance of differences: Andy, solid, practical, good with his hands, forever building something, Harry constantly drifting to the metaphysical, the speculative. And yet, their friendship persisted.

Teresa.

She was anarchy, the barbarian at the gate, the invasion that threatened to destroy, to tear apart the fabric of everything. Her life before this was enigmatic: recruited straight from university, never any reference to her past except for several career shifts, from academia, the law, the environment and now to this business; a relentless pursuit Harry felt, of something, anything that gave her control.

Harry stood, his attention drawn as always, to the large window at the side of Andy's office, to the sparkling waters of the harbour beneath the arch of the bridge. Small sailing boats leaned precariously away from a blustery nor'easter, dodging ferries, cruise liners and container ships. Harry wondered how people found the time to play on the harbour pond during the week.

Love could turn into hate with such ease. Harry had believed that it was love, a desperate hope that buried him beneath another's will, submitted him to nothingness – laziness, he realised, wanting a presentable solution, neat, tidy, acceptable. What could go wrong? They were the perfect pair. The future was assured.

'Harry.'

The hum of the office air-con.

'Harry!' Andy raised his voice.

Harry twisted away from the harbour view. 'It looks good on the harbour,' he said.

Andy looked frustrated. 'You've had too much time away, Harry. You need to get your focus back.'

Focus.

Harry reckoned his focus was just fine. Finally, he was moving in the right direction.

'We need you to get moving on the North African project. They need some solid organisation, preferably you in Tunis.'

Harry was quiet, finally saying, 'Andy, are you trying to get me out of here?'

Andy's turn for a pause.

'Clever you. Harry, you do need to get out of here. You've been contemplating your navel for weeks now. You're a bloody vulnerable bastard, and here, you're knee-deep in personal shit.'

'I'm fine!' The personal intrusion, even from Andy, rankled.

'It's all sorted.'

'Sorted! She's been telling everyone you're getting married!'

'It's sorted, Andy. I've talked to Teresa. She's accepted the truth of it.'

'And what's the truth, Harry?'

'It's not going to happen. She realises that, now.'

'Harry, you're a bloody fool.'

'We had a discussion, and I believe she's accepted the *no-go*.'

'The *no-go*?'

'Yeah, she's not getting what she wants!'

'Harry, wake up. Teresa is relentless. She'll never give up as long as you are around, and even with you gone won't necessarily stop her.'

Harry was silent. He recognised the truth in Andy's words.

'She said you've got problems with the board,' Harry said. He wanted to divert the conversation to other matters.

'Yes, there are always problems with the board,' Andy said. 'They're a bunch of know-alls, full of advice, nothing I can't handle. The point is, we need you in Tunis, and you need to get out of here.' Harry heard genuine concern in Andy's voice.

'All right.' Harry acquiesced; Andy's grasp of reality was irrefutable. 'Give me a few weeks to wind things up here.'

'What? You mean this search you've been on?'

'Yeah, that and things with Frances.'

Andy nodded, a signal that the conversation was ended. Harry turned to the exit, glancing once again through the window. The north wind had strengthened, the tiny sails were retreating to the lee shore, a grey hawk swooped amongst the tall buildings, plummeting to the street far below. Harry resisted the urge to closely follow its flight. He stopped at the door, turning back to Andy. 'Just a few weeks, Andy. There are urgent things that need to be done.'

Andy nodded again. 'Tell me when you're ready to go,' he said, glancing up from the papers on his desk. 'And don't worry about Teresa. She'll be up to her eyeballs taking care of things here, so she won't have time for anything else for a while – give you a chance to escape.'

Escape?

There was no escape! A getaway from what? From his mistakes, his responsibilities, from the possibility of getting it right, doing the right thing? In such a short time, things had changed so much. Now, running was impossible; the demons must be met, fears subdued.

*

Tweeting birds.

Harry dragged the phone from his pocket.

Submerged in static noise, a distant voice said, 'Harry,' so faint that Harry stopped breathing, the rush of air to his lungs threatening to overwhelm the faint voice.

'Yes. This is Harry.'

Static pulsed, fierce, so severe Harry was forced to pull the phone away from his ear.

'Yes,' he said again, clamping the phone hard against his head, voice raised against the noise, a finger plugging the opposite ear against the clamour of the city traffic. 'Harry, here.'

He thought he heard a response buried beneath the static hiss. The voice sounded female, but he wasn't sure, the word *wait* emerging from the chaotic noise. Wait! For what? Yet, he persisted, the phone growing hot against his ear.

The static pulsed again then subsided.

'Are you there?'

'Yes!' Harry felt his heart leap. 'Yes, Anika, I'm here. Where are you?'

'Not much time. The battery's running low. We survived, Harry.'

'Where are you, Anika? Where have you been?'

'Cut off. Everything destroyed. We've been living under branches from a fallen tree for over a week. Almost didn't make it away from the storm surge. We can talk about it when I get to Dhaka. But, I'm all right, and everyone here has been so helpful and kind.'

'Anika, when in Dhaka?'

'Just a few days, maybe less. We're driving from here. The roads and traffic are bad, worse now because of the storm damage.' Harry remembered the chaos of the Bangladesh roads, the constant avoidance of careering buses and trucks, the weaving drive around road washouts, the masses of people crowding along the roadside.

'Ring me when you can,' Harry said. 'I need to know you're safe.' He waited for a response, eventually realising that the static was gone, the connection severed – such tenuous links served to amplify his need, the presence he so desired.

Harry walked briskly towards the hotel, barely suppressing the elation he felt: alive, safe, wanting to talk to him, seeking him out amidst the chaos. Images of Anika's journey towards Dhaka played in his mind – the pressure of population, the weight of storm-borne dislocation, the disintegration of fragile infrastructure. He knew destructive events were familiar to the delta people, their acceptance of absence rather than existence summarising their life at the margins of humanity – affluence seemed to breed disaffection, privation, a *make-do* view.

Suddenly the blaring of a horn – a familiar, relentless noise on the roads about Dhaka.

Ignore it!

The noise persisted.

Just a cultural need – lean on your car horn, be heard, be noticed.

The screech of tyres – Harry looked up, realising he had walked onto the busy road.

A large vehicle slewed as it braked, uncontrolled, Harry watching, fascinated with its approach, wondering whether this would end his days. How had it come to this? Simple negligence leading to the cessation of everything.

The vehicle continued its sliding path.

Harry couldn't move – was this his death wish?

Still sliding.

Harry closed his eyes, held his breath, waited for the impact. At least he had talked to Anika one last time.

Nothing.

Eyes open, he stared at the driver of the stationary vehicle – an attractive, young woman, twenty-something – pale face contorted with distress. Harry placed his hands, palm down, on the hood, breathed deeply, walking to the driver's window.

'I'm so sorry,' she said. 'I've had such a day. I wasn't concentrating.'

Focus, Harry thought exhaling loudly, *sometimes a blessing, often a curse.*

'Yes, it's been quite a day,' he said. 'I wasn't quite with it either.'

He turned to go, then stopped, and said, 'Great driving by the way. I appreciate it. Gold star for reactions.'

He walked, more attentively now, remembering the final moment of his interview with Teresa. It had not ended well. Tears had turned to sullenness, petulance to hostility, anger to outright aggression. Teresa could not grasp the concept of free will, the idea that Harry would want intimacy with anyone but herself.

'But why?' Teresa kept reciting the mantra. 'We're perfect for each other.' The words struck Harry as an affirmation of Teresa's absolute belief in her own judgement: she had found a *perfect*, pliant sperm donor, and nothing would shift her from her self-belief.

Eventually, the phone tweeted, Teresa annoyed at the interruption. It was a message from his mother, and through the annoyance, Teresa's parting jibe oddly gave him hope that maybe the realities of the situation were finally penetrating the egotistic wall. 'Well, I'm not going to beg,' she said. 'This is an opportunity for us both, and we shouldn't squander it.'

Harry felt the familiar pang of doubt at the words: was his judgement correct, was this an opportunity too good to miss, and his hopes with Anika's misguided foolery that would leave him bereft of a future?

He walked away from Teresa, though, with a sense of relief.

Maybe this was freedom from the vice that had gripped him so firmly. Now perhaps, he could follow an unfettered path? A sense of freedom washed about him until, with a feeling of dismay, he recalled his mother's words.

Harry, come home as soon as you can. Frances and the baby are in trouble and need your help.

Dubious but dutiful, Harry rang his mother as he walked, expecting the typical harangue, an exposition of his shortcomings, advice on what he needed to do to restore his standing, and he wasn't disappointed.

'Harry, you need to front up and take responsibility for your actions,' Ruth said.

'What actions specifically, Mum?' Harry felt worn down by circumstance.

'Frances and the baby, what else?'

'Mum, Frances has washed her hands of me. She basically told me to bugger off.'

'She doesn't mean that, Harry.'

'Mum, what's happened.'

A pause, the sound of exhaled breath – frustration, irritation or indecision? Harry guessed she was fabricating some exaggeration, an embellishment calculated to mobilise him in the desired direction.

'Frances. She's in hospital.'

Harry waited silently for the follow-up, for the proclamation that would rally him to his mother's wishes. When the silence lengthened to an uncomfortable interlude, he submitted. 'Why, Mum. Why's she in hospital?'

The gap extended until he felt the silence could no longer be endured.

At last, 'Harry.' He heard the distress in her voice; was that a sob? 'It's cancer.'

Shit! Unrequited ex-lovers, now the critically ill. The thought choked at its source – disingenuous, unkind, ill-tempered, even narcissistic.

'Mum, what sort?'

'Breast, but it's gone too far.'

'Too far? What does that mean?'

'Not just the breast anymore.'

'Bloody hell. Which hospital?' It could no longer be a standoff – he had to acknowledge the relationship, the connection with the past, their link to the future, the bond that couldn't be ignored. 'And who's looking after the kid?'

'The little one is fine, Harry,' Ruth said. 'I'm looking after her.'

Harry wasn't sure about the "fine" bit, at least not with his mother in the long term. The fears and phobias she had instilled in him weren't a recommendation for her parenting skills.

'Where is she, Mum?'

'Royal North Shore.'

Harry headed for his car – first his mother, then Frances. He had to try to put things to rights, no matter how belatedly – he had to try.

*

Ruth's place always had a slightly dilapidated feel about it – not derelict, not run-down; instead, its state was a consequence, Harry thought, of the city, the grime of millions of people, the traffic, the humidity and his mother's propensity for old – hanging onto things because they meant something, something past rather than present.

Harry parked the car on the steep drive, pulled open the cast-iron gate, wandering down the narrow passageway leading to the rear of the house. The sound of an interviewed celebrity, politician or similar identity issued from a television on the veranda, alternately petulant, argumentative, coercive.

'Dad!' Harry said, voice raised above the blare of the interview.

'Son,' said a man looking up from the glare of the television, from within an oversized padded chair that seemed to fold about his body. 'Fancy seeing you here.'

A pause while the interview reached its crescendo.

Harry's father said, dragging his eyes from the screen, 'Looking for your mother?'

Harry stood mute for a moment in the flickering TV light, reflecting on the aptness of his father's response: this *was* a rare visit, a place he chose to avoid; and this *was* the sum total, it seemed, of any conversation with his father – quickly passed on to his mother in case some critical detail or opinion was missed. 'Yeah, Dad. Is she around?'

'Somewhere in the house. Go look.' Attention immediately returned to the video commentary.

A small step up into the loungeroom, past the old fireplace – he'd never seen a fire in that hearth – through to the third bedroom that served as a study. Ruth sat at a desk, dark hazel eyes distressed, blinking back tears. 'Harry. I thought that was you. Why are you here?'

Why? He wondered that himself. Could a conversation with his mother benefit anyone? Would she listen, adapt, work cooperatively towards a resolution?

Harry moved to get a better view of the garden through the window. The unkempt lawn, then a brick wall, a bulwark against the busy road below, corrugated-iron sheeting covering the hole Ruth called *the grave*, used to pit-fire her pots until the introduction of a permanent total fire ban. Now just a forgotten remnant, an odd reminder of halcyon days.

Halcyon days? He reckoned they were a figment of their collective imagination – things had always been in turmoil.

'So much to do,' Ruth said, a hopeless, helpless tone.

'Things will get better,' he said, looking at Ruth, instantly regretting the sickly platitude. They had to try, but sprouting inanities wouldn't get them there.

'They would,' she said, 'if you just stayed put for a while and fronted up to your responsibilities.' Ruth, forever the blunt realist.

Harry looked away to the ceiling, noticing for the first time the store of spiderwebs, the accumulated neglect where Ruth had once scrubbed away even the hint of dilapidation. Time was weighing heavily on this place, on his parents' enthusiasm for life, the message suddenly clear.

Harry turned and looked at Ruth. Her face was rigid, colour suffusing drawn cheeks, and her emotions threatened to break free from rheumy eyes. Her eyes met Harry.

'That's why I'm here,' said Harry.

'Well, you'd better do something for a change,' Ruth was tired, just wanting to be relieved of the burden, 'like taking charge of Sofie.'

'Living in a hotel and always in temporary digs isn't conducive to raring a child, Mum.' As he uttered the words, Harry saw the thinness of his response.

'Harry ...' Ruth launching her counterattack.

Harry cut her off. 'Yeah, I know, Mum. *I've got to front up to my responsibilities.*' Ruth was getting irritatingly repetitive.

'And soon. In fact, right now!' Ruth's clenched fist struck the table.

Harry nodded. 'Yeah.' The need was obvious, what to do not so clear. 'Thought I would talk to you before seeing Frances.'

'Talking to me is just delaying what you know you should be doing.'

'What's that, Mum? What should I be doing?' He couldn't help revealing the irritation he felt, a lifetime critical of his every decision.

Ruth drew a deep breath. Was that exasperation or just a need to gather strength? 'First Frances, then Sofie, the product of your caprice.'

Capricious was a curious way to describe his life: evasive perhaps, particularly when faced with personalities that tried to dominate, those who attempted to plot his path – Ruth, Teresa, even Frances. His instinct was to rebel, a matter of survival really, take another way, any other direction, escape, run. He felt it now, the desire to be rid of responsibility for others, to run to where the routine of work would deny the intimate intrusion of others.

'So, where is she? You said you were looking after her?' said Harry.

'Day care,' Ruth said. 'Just the afternoon. I'll go and get her soon. You should come.'

Harry debated the need to be at the pickup. Would refusal be just another attempt to run away, a perpetuation of his flight from responsibility?

'No,' he said. 'I need to see Frances at the hospital, before it gets too late.'

Harry took a deep breath. He could see Ruth's disappointment slip into irritation. He leant forward on the small lounge opposite Ruth, elbows propped on his knees, chin resting on hands. He could predict her judgement, never easy to hear, least of all to accept. He waited for the inevitable torrent of advice, realising that argument now would just polarise opinion, solving nothing.

Ruth obliged.

'Frances needs your support, now more than ever,' Ruth said, 'and so does Sofie.' She closed her eyes as she talked, looking older that way, the lines about her eyes revealing fatigue usually concealed by constant activity, by her relentless assault on life. 'You need to commit to supporting them both.'

'Mum, she told me to bugger off, so ...'

Eyes open. 'Listen, for once in your life, Harry, listen.' Ruth stopped, glaring savagely at Harry. 'She did that because you couldn't be relied upon. Go and tell her that you're a changed person, that you love her, and you'll stand by her.' Desperation saturated Ruth's voice.

Harry nodded. He knew that Frances would hardly be swayed by such a convenient statement, yet in a way, Ruth was right. It was clear where his responsibility lay.

He walked back to his car, through a house succumbing to the late afternoon gloom, noticing for the first time the slight damp odour that emanated from moist floors and foundations – signs of physical deterioration, the passage of time, encroaching neglect. His responsibilities dwelt, he realised, beyond the here and now.

He breathed deeply as he climbed into the rented vehicle looking at the backs of his hands, at the signs of sun damage from years of surfing, and deterioration in the pattern of veins. His mother had talked sense – impossible wishful thinking perhaps, but understandable in a world that seemed to be crumbling.

Turn the key, drive through frantic evening traffic, seek recovery in the face of terrible odds.

CHAPTER 17

September 5

Harry stepped across the threshold through an entrance that looked more like a hotel than the largest hospital in Sydney. *Who are they kidding?* he thought. *The sick and dying are here, not tourists and vacationers.* He scanned the foyer and located the information desk, approaching an attractive young woman who beamed a welcoming smile.

'Yes, how may I help you?'

Harry almost responded with: *Yeah, it's been a hard-drinking week. I need a new liver. Got one?* He subdued his sarcasm, asking instead for Frances.

The receptionist focused on the computer screen before her, tapping vaguely for a moment at a keyboard, then said, looking up at Harry, 'Take the lifts to your right, third floor, ask for directions at the nurses' aid station.'

Harry thanked her, turning towards a cluster of people waiting for the arrival of an elevator. *Like waiting for ascension to heaven*, he thought, *a bit presumptuous really, all of us expecting to go up, not down*, then discarded the sentiment as too cynical, too morose – he knew positivity was needed for what was to come, that he needed to rehearse the right attitude, to project optimism rather than futility.

The lift arrived, the crowd surged forward, Harry almost abandoning the effort to board – *might buy time*, he thought, *have a coffee at that funky little café in the foyer, gather myself, work out the words to say.*

He hesitated, ready to turn, to run once again. The jostling pack pushed him forward into the lift; their choice now, their decision to ascend was irresistible. The tiny cubicle filled behind, jostling him to the car's rear. Choice gone, he thrust his arm through the throng, reaching, pressing number three as the doors hissed together, a gentle shudder, the supplicants heading, not down but to the heavens.

So disturbing, he thought as he walked up to the ward desk, *the electronic air of a hospital, its sterility, impotence, the tension of the inhabitants* – memories of his grandfather's final hospital moments almost made him turn again and run.

The ward nurse gave him Frances' location, pointing along the corridor before bustling away on some more important task. A long trek to the far end, a sharp right turn into a clinical, austere room, one of those mechanically embellished hospital beds in the far corner by a window that overlooked a car park. Frances was gazing absently through the window, sitting upright on the bed, her back propped against massed pillows, legs stretched out, hospital gown riding above her knees.

Harry stood in the doorway for a moment, assimilating the scene. Strangely, Frances looked well, for he had expected a significant decline. *Was that his morbid view of the world dictating outcomes*? Maybe Ruth's prognosis was a cruel extension of her desire for drama?

'Frances,' Harry said.

Frances' eyes swung to Harry, without expression, it seemed without recognition. For a moment, she observed him quietly.

'Harry,' Frances said at last. 'What are you doing here?'

Harry felt that Frances and Ruth had perhaps choreographed their responses. *Was he such an unexpected, shocking visitor in people's lives that they needed to coordinate their response to his possible arrival?*

'Ruth told me you were unwell.'

Silence.

Frances drew a breath, the rush of air making a whistling sound. 'Yes, you could say that, Harry.'

Silence again. It was like the conversation had ended, almost before it had begun.

'Well, she told me it was rather more serious than just unwell,' he added limply. No use beating about the bush. What could, should he say? *You'll be okay? Everything will be alright?* Everything would not be okay. So, he just stood there, feeling foolish, feeling like the bastard he was, the deserter.

Eventually, Frances said, 'Harry, we all have to die. I'm just going a little earlier than most.'

All he could do was stand mute, eyes down, observing the shabbiness of his shoes, inwardly dealing with his culpability, self-reproach that gave him no leeway for escape.

'But you'll have to step up, take responsibility for Sofie. I won't be here to pick her up when she falls,' Frances said with a slightly husky voice. Harry looked up; distress, no, it was grief reflected in Frances' eyes. 'I won't get to see her grow. You'll have to do that for me.'

Harry nodded, unsettled by the weight of Frances' expectations – a life now his responsibility.

'Mum said she'd take Sofie,' Harry said, almost to himself, half said, half meant.

Frances closed her eyes and shook her head. 'Harry, she means well, but it would be too much for her. And your dad is no use to himself, let alone anyone else.'

A silent moment, Frances' eyes open, fixed on Harry, her stare willing him to respond.

She was right. The shabbiness of Ruth's house and the weariness he had seen weren't passing anomalies. Where else could the remains of Frances' life reside, their creation, a life?

Harry nodded again. No choice, no dodging obligation, no rejecting responsibility, no placing the burden in the hands of others.

'Yes. Mine,' he said. 'My responsibility.' It was a vow that seemed to float before him.

Harry watched the tension leave Frances, a slight smile passing across her pale lips.

'Have you been talking to mum?' he said as a thought came to him.

'Yes, Harry. I talk to Ruth every day.'

'Today?'

Frances smiled again. 'Yes. She phoned to say you were on your way here.'

*

A slow walk to the train, North Sydney Station, with the memory of his student days commuting on the noisy, old red-rattler carriages that plied the city rail system in those days, windows that never completely closed, the seats you swung this way or that to sit facing forward or back, the smell of ozone from the flickering overhead electric cables. He moved with the crowd aboard the modern carriage, clean, air-conditioned, insulated from the city's dirt, heading across the bridge to meet the teeming horde as it flowed from offices into the narrow streets and laneways, homeward bound after another tedious day.

The hospital's clinical sterility and Frances' plight still clung to Harry, the inevitability of everything, a downward spiral, disintegration that seemed to catch everyone from birth. What part did fate play in destiny, in the outcome?

He shook his head, trying to clear away the build-up of fuzziness that seemed to come after such heavy conversations. He remembered his grandfather's last moments, the words: *made decisions, then felt guilty. Never knew what I really wanted, lost myself, my family.* They were words that triggered this fateful journey into the lives of others. He now realised that everyone was bound to the past by a legacy of deeply felt emotions. The constant dysphoria that was his life was not his making, not anyone's making, just the by-product of the journey through life and the experiences that created the person.

The train paused at Milsons Point, the northern gateway to the bridge. Harry watched a young woman with a large backpack alight from the train, trudging towards the exit stairs. *No doubt, off to some cheap digs*, he thought, *another temporary resting place before moving on to the next point in a nomadic evolution.* He wondered whether he had allowed others to dictate too much of his life's outcomes. *A bit hard to tell how much influence the past had exerted on choice.* All he could think was: *I have reached this point, good or bad, and now is the time to apply some direct thought to a confrontation with the future.*

Backpacker gone, drawn downward to her uncertain future, the carriage rolled forward, onto the approaches to the bridge, past the North Sydney pool below to the right, a pond clinging to the harbour edge, the riveted steel arch towering above the bustling harbour. Harry waited for his own descent through the gaping maw of the tunnel leading to the Wynyard Station, holding his breath in the first few seconds – this subterranean passage always filled him with unease, the same apprehension he had felt crawling into Jimmy's cave – the fusty smell of a small space where air stagnated, and sunlight was excluded. Was this reaction more evidence of the power of the past?

The walk was long up the busy Wynyard ramp to George Street, pushing through the resolute commuters as they bustled down towards their escape route; his goal – fresh air and sunlight – was diminished in the late afternoon by the forest of office towers that cast deep shadows into the city canyons, but Harry didn't mind – the air was clean, his next steps along the winding path now clear.

Without further reflection, his resolve releasing the tight knot in his stomach, Harry increased his pace, almost breaking into a run as he neared the hotel. Frances' voice was in his head, soft, reasonable, logical despite her dilemma:

Harry, she means well, but it would be too much for her. And your dad is no use to himself, let alone anyone else.

Harry knew now he had the determination to accept responsibility for his missteps, to work from the heart, with the ability and constancy to take charge. He knew it when Frances, despite her death sentence, showed such deep concern for Sofie and could see the impossible burden this all placed on Ruth.

Once again, he dropped, phone in hand, into one of the hotel foyer chairs and rang.

The buzz of the call. The click of a connection.

'Mum. I'm coming to pick up Sofie. Be there in an hour.'

'Harry, you can't take her now. We're just getting dinner, then she's off to her bath and bed.'

Harry paused, gathering together an image of preparations for dinner and bed, remembering the tumult of his childhood: Ruth shouting instructions, the vegetables turning to a tasteless, watery pulp as they boiled away on the stove, his father barely home from the city commute, desperately absorbed in the TV news.

Of course, she was right! He had a lot to remember, a lot to relearn.

'Tomorrow morning, then.' This had to be the last compromise.

Silence. A deep breath. Was Ruth irritated or relieved?

'Okay, Harry. I guess you know what you're doing.'

Despite his fresh resolve, Harry wondered where this was taking him.

*

Andy answered his phone, shouting through what seemed like the end of a windy tunnel, a wet, blustery shaft, muffled yells in the background.

'We'll be back at the club soon,' he said. 'In the next hour. We can talk then. Can't risk getting this phone drenched right now. It's pretty blowie out here.'

'It's the middle of the week, Andy. Shouldn't you be in the office?'

'Invited. You can't let a chance for a turn on one of these big mothers get away.'

'Sounds like a tough gig.'

'Plenty to get sea-sick with out here. Mountainous seas.'

Another shout, more urgent this time. 'Gotta go, Harry. Talk soon.' The line cut.

Harry doubted the mountainous bit. It was like that universal surfer's exaggeration: 'The swell's small today, but you should have seen it yesterday!'

Harry sat at the edge of the hotel lobby settee, the music from the piano near the bar reverberating from the vaulted ceiling. Places like this projected a fabricated vitality, forced animation designed to immerse the client in an alien world that disavowed reality, the chaos beyond the front door.

Thirst.

Harry was succumbing to the strands of the distant amorphous composition.

He headed towards the source of the refrain, scanning the crowded lobby for a familiar face. Eventually, with no familiarity in the gathering, he perched precariously on one of the elevated seats at the bar.

'A dry white, thanks,' he said as the barman approached, recalling the first sip of wine at the club in Dhaka, the subtle blend of cooking wine and boiled alcohol – a staple diet of rehydrating beer from that first taste. The Chittagong docks were the demise of many good vintages.

Harry raised the glass, observing its rich colour, the hotel lights glancing off the fluid. He paused, the wine glass held aloft, thinking of Frances' dire predicament, how his commitment meant such a profound departure from the path of all his years. He saw Anika's face in the wine glow and wondered what path she followed, whether the chaos of her life would lead her to him again. Nothing was guaranteed, nothing could be predicted with any certainty, nothing was a forgone conclusion. Frances might survive, miracles did happen, good endings were not verboten – and he might be reunited with Anika.

Birds tweeting.

Harry dug into his pocket.

'Yeah, Harry here.'

'Harry, Andy.'

'They've released you from servitude before the mast, have they.'

'Bloody hard work, mate, pulling on those lines, raising and lowering the main and jib sheets, forever cleating and trimming the sheets and lines ...'

'Sounds like your part of the crew now, Andy. An old salt.'

'Enough of the sarcasm. What's happening.'

Harry took a deep breath. 'Andy, I've decided to quit.'

Silence. Just Andy's breathing.

Harry filled the gap. 'Did you hear me, Andy?'

'Yeah, yeah, I heard you. And where did this bright idea come from?'

'Andy, it's the whole mess. Frances needs support, the kid needs looking after, and you don't need me in Tunis or anywhere. There are plenty of people who can carry that one forward.'

'Shit. Harry, you've always underrated yourself. Has Teresa had a go at you again?'

'No. Andy, no! This is something that needs to be dealt with by me. More than that, Frances, Sofie, and even mum, desperately need help. There's no one else. And while I'm doing that, I can't give the job what it deserves. It wouldn't be fair on you or everyone else here or in Tunis.'

'You're fixed on this, then?' A tone of resignation was creeping into Andy's voice.

'Yeah. I had hoped we could have a beer or something and tell you face to face.'

'Where are you? I mean, now.'

'The hotel, in the bar, waiting for Godot.'

'Stay there. I'm on my way. Thirty minutes. Don't get pissed before I get there.'

Get pissed? Those days were gone. Depending on how tired he was, one or two drinks were enough. He swirled the wine in the glass, examining the whirlpool, realising that it formed an odd metaphor for his life, turbulence that tossed him from one calamity to another – his doing, most of it, a chain he had wrapped about himself, a weight that seemed to drag him into the mire, the mess of emotions, the hunger and thirst of others, despite his best attempts at dispassion, detachment, impartiality.

Bird tweeting again. Andy changing his mind?

'Yeah, Harry here.'

'Harry.' The voice was loud and clear. Harry set the glass carefully on the bar.

'Anika.'

'Where are you?' she said.

'Hotel.' The word caught in a suddenly parched throat. 'I'm at the hotel here in Sydney. Where are you?'

'Airport. Dhaka. On my way to Sydney.'

'When? What's your ETA?'

'A short stop in Singapore to tell the NGO I'm leaving. I'm leaving Bangladesh. I'll arrive in a day or so. I have to go. They're calling the flight.'

Harry's words seemed to lose their way from his brain to mouth, elation mixed with trepidation. Finally, he said, 'Send me the flight details!'

'Have to go. See you in Sydney.' The line went dead.

'Harry.'

Harry turned to a red-faced Andy. Had it been thirty minutes? He looked at his friend, suddenly aware of the change wrought by the years, Andy's growing paunch – too many long lunches? The pressure of corporate survival played on Andy's face. Harry glanced down briefly at his own gut, a bump edging into prominence.

'Nice to see you, Andy. In a hurry?'

'Mate, you level that "I'm quitting" line at me, and yeah, I'm in a hurry.' Andy's eyes lifted to the bar. 'Same as him,' he said to the barman, pointing to Harry's glass.

Harry took a deep breath. If this was going to be a hard word session, it would be a long night. 'I need to do this, Andy. Frances is in trouble, and the kid needs looking after.' He thought of Anika's imminent arrival amidst the mess of these new responsibilities – would their relationship survive?

'How bad? I mean Frances,' Andy said as he lifted a full glass from the bar, taking a lingering draft, eyes never leaving Harry.

'Bad, doctors say weeks, a month at best.'

Andy winced. 'No getting past it,' he said, resignation flooding his voice. 'You need to be here to deal with all this.'

'I can't just bugger off to the Med or someplace. Not now.'

'Yeah, I see that.'

'And there's Anika.'

'Yeah, Anika, the Bangladeshi bird you've fallen in love with.'

'She's American, and I'm not sure about the "in-love" bit.'

'Mate, you've been moping about for weeks. It's been *Anika this* and *Anika that*.'

Harry recognised the tactic: *Agree with the sentiment, deflect the argument*. 'She's on her way to Sydney right now.'

'Now that's gotta be love.'

'What do you mean, *gotta be*?'

'Coming here, to you, with all these complications swirling around you.'

Harry was silent for a moment. Was that a rat he smelt – a very dead rat? Finally, he said, 'You knew she was coming?'

'Just a guess, Harry.'

'No, you knew! You've been talking to her.'

'Well, yeah. We've been setting up the aid programme for the Sundarbans and ...'

'... and you just happened to involve yourself in my relationship!' Harry felt a flush of resentment.

'No, it wasn't meddling, Harry. She just wanted to know how things were with you here. So, I told her.'

'Told her what?' Suspicion was on the rise.

'That you were off bashing around the bush looking for a ghost, you were fending off a rampant suiter, and you were trying to make amends for abandoning a former lover and your child.'

Harry sat stunned for a moment. Finally, 'You said that?'

Andy smiled a wry grin. 'No, but we did talk about what you were doing, and she put two and two together. She's one smart lady. No chance of *you* pulling the wool over *her* eyes.'

It was the truth, but Harry baulked at the fact – too many failures because he had run from the truth.

'Then why is she heading this way?'

Andy leant forward, placing a hand on Harry's shoulder, a mollifying manoeuvre? 'Maybe she sees something in you that the rest of us don't.'

Andy continued to smile, softer now. Was that pity Harry saw?

'Look, Harry, we've known each other for how long?' Andy paused, seeming to consider the years. 'Is it twenty-five years? Maybe more? And in that time, we've built this business, the company, into a competitive unit. Both of us have played our part and developed our roles. We're sharper than the majors. We can move faster onto opportunities. No red tape, no endless lines of management to go through for approval, no wankers diverting us into meaningless drivel.'

Harry cut into Andy's diatribe. 'Fine. But what's your point, Andy?'

Andy took a breath. 'I have a proposal for you.'

'What? That I ignore the distress of my family and sacrifice myself on your business altar?'

'No! Not at all. My proposal is ...' Another breath, deeper this time, '... that we swap roles for a time. I take care of the North African ventures. You look after the board and the investors.'

'Andy, do you seriously want to unleash me on such a sensitive mob as the board and the investors?'

'Listen, Harry, I've seen you successfully negotiate with some devious shit and come out smelling like roses. And it would mean you are based here, not in some god-forsaken corner of the world. We can adjust to some other arrangement when things have been resolved here.'

Harry was silent for a moment. He pondered Andy's skill at turning a situation on its head, at pushing, particularly him, into a logical corner.

'I'll think about it,' Harry said, as a delaying strategy, though he wondered what a deferred decision would achieve.

'Not too long,' said Andy. 'The North Africa thing needs a kick, and Anika is arriving tomorrow, and she is expecting *fait accompli* on this.'

Harry saw the rat.

'You talked specifically about this with Anika,' said Harry, ready to lash out.

'Yeah, this possible scenario did come up,' Andy said with a grin. 'But it was entirely her decision to head this way.'

Manipulation! Was he a victim or a beneficiary? Did it matter? Anika would arrive, and he would have a chance at happiness and maybe even redemption.

CHAPTER 18

September 6

'So, where are you going to live, Harry? She needs somewhere stable, not hotel rooms and bars in some foreign place rife with slavers and refugees.' Ruth was standing her ground.

'I've got an apartment.'

'And during the day, when you're at work?'

'I can afford a minder, a nursie,' he said.

'And there's school!' Ruth's objections were endless. Never mind, it would be years before real school became a consuming event.

'She can go to boarding school,' he said. 'They take them really young.'

'No! Harry! You can't mean that! It will ruin her. She'll end up like those poor wretches abandoned in the dormitory by their parents, to the torments of Dickensian cruelty and prejudice.'

'No, Mum.' Harry regretted his levity. 'I wouldn't do that.'

'She needs a mother.' Bitterness, a finality in Ruth's words.

Harry bit back the obvious retort: *Well, there won't be one, she'll be dead*, instead saying, 'Who knows, Mum, Frances might pull through. They *are* trying out some pretty radical treatments.'

Ruth shook her head, eyes downcast, tight-lipped, turning away towards the kitchen, muttering something that might have been: *Pigs might fly.*

Harry followed her, feeling unsure despite his outward show, powerless to alter the fateful course, the advance of delinquent cells, the immersion of himself in the lives of others. Ruth's bitter polemic did not relieve the uneasiness.

'Clothes, a few toys, and her favourite blanket. Where are you staying tonight?' Ruth leafed through a small pile of belongings perched on the kitchen bench, finally raising her eyes, staring at Harry, accusative, anger brushing close to the surface.

'Mum, I have to be at the airport.' Harry didn't have time for further recriminations. 'Thanks for all your help. We'll be stopping by the hospital on the way.' He grabbed the tiny bundle of possessions, bending to scoop up the child on the floor, a movement that strained his back – was he too old for this caper?

He took the car, wishing he had the old Land Cruiser, something to bully his way through the manic evening traffic, protection against the aggression prevalent these days on Sydney roads. Sofie gurgled. *Good kid*, he thought as he glanced sideways at the child. *She's enjoying the ride, the here and now, the stupidity of all these drivers, with no promises, no disappointments.*

Park the car, straight to the ward this time, Harry, the veteran of hospitals, taking the kid to see the infirmed – a final goodbye or celebration of a reprieve?

'I don't want to be here anymore, Harry!'

What could he say? *Right. Pack your bag. We'll go now.*

'Yeah, but you're in the middle of treatment,' he said, regretting the unhelpful response.

'They give me less than thirty per cent chance,' said Frances as she absently caressed Sophie, the despair in her eyes softening as amused murmurs rose from the child. 'I don't want to spend my remaining days locked away here.'

Harry felt the clinical sterility of the place rush at him, the impotence of existence in such a place – indeed, it was enough to shorten life just being here.

Sophie squeaked, hands beating against the blankets that shrouded Frances' legs.

A smile. When had Harry last seen Frances smile? He couldn't remember.

Clatter as the door swung open, a trolley was shoved vigorously into the room by a nurse draped in a protective gown. 'Time for your infusion,' the nurse said. 'I'm afraid your visitors will have to leave.'

Harry looked at Frances, despondency returning to her face, resignation as she gently pushed Sophie towards Harry.

As the image of the hospital's clinical necessities receded near the airport, Harry's thoughts swerved to the here and now, to the imminent meeting, a reunion. In fact, he wondered at the sense of it, given his promises, commitments, and vows, like some sort of priest, a fallen cleric staggering towards redemption. He laughed despite the seriousness of everything, almost sour, but not entirely – he was a hopeless case, wanting things to be correct and positively resolved – thirty per cent wasn't zero; Anika might embrace his recent acquisition. He glanced briefly at Sophie, his profound charge.

'Come on,' he said as he lifted Sophie from the child seat, turning as he pushed the door closed. 'There's someone I'd like you to meet.'

They hurried across the airport forecourt, dodging taxis that sped away from the kerb to line up for another fare. Through the doors, into the arrival hall – Sydney's Mascot Airport always made him feel claustrophobic; organically grown, a bit here, a bit there, accidental logic, convenient, compromised design. He saw the crowd milling about the immigration and customs exit.

Harry glanced at his watch, then at the arrivals screen; the flight was past due. Suddenly he felt apprehensive – he hadn't wanted it this way. It was unfair to expect a positive response; dying ex-lover, baby. He had no right to demand her commitment to his mess, an involvement that he had only just accepted.

He watched the occasional dishevelled traveller stagger through the exit, most pushing trolleys laden with mountains of luggage, their eyes scanning for familiar faces within the expectant horde.

Another glance at his watch. Maybe she had missed the connection to Sydney. Had he misread the details, the time, her message?

Arriving Tuesday from Singapore, 10am your time.

That was all, no further detail. Her messages were always short, almost cryptic, his reply asking for more information unanswered. He dragged the phone from its burial in a deep trouser pocket, transferring Sophie to his right side, fumbling with his finger to the stored message.

Confirmed. He had the right day, the right time.

Another glance at the arrivals screen.

Landed!

'Hello, Harry.'

Anika stood before him, dressed like a long-distance traveller: loose-fitting, grey tracksuit top and pants, shoes that looked like slippers, a small messenger bag over the right shoulder, towing a single cabin trolley case. Harry had never seen her dressed for travel, only in work or holiday gear: lace-up boots, mud-splattered trousers at one extreme, beach wear at the other. Despite obvious fatigue, Harry was immediately lost in her allure.

Before words could find their way to Harry's mouth, Anika released the trailing bag and stepped close, kissing him, long, lingering, moist eyes closed, an arm wrapped about his back, holding their bodies tightly together. Separation came suddenly, pushed away to arm's length.

'And who is this?' Anika said, smiling, gently touching Sophie's leg.

Anxiety returning, Harry swallowed. 'This is Sophie.' He had to say it; no room for obfuscation. 'My daughter.'

Anika was silent for a moment, her attention firmly riveted on the child. 'Yes. I can see the resemblance. She has your eyes.' Anika's eyes eventually turned to Harry, her attention renewing his apprehension, his eyes pressed into a wary squint.

'Welcome to Sydney,' he said, attempting a degree of formality despite the lingering, tingling sensation on his lips. 'Is that all your luggage?'

A stupid question instantly regretted.

'Yes. Nothing else coming,' she said, a ghost of a smile passing briefly across her face.

'You're not surprised?' Harry needed to know how she felt.

Harry was held by Anika's eyes, quiet. Was that softness or resignation?

Anika shook her head. 'You've been busy, Harry,' she said, with Harry transfixed by her perfect, white, even teeth, moist lips, a smile absorbed by her delectable mouth.

'Busy?' he said, emerging at last from thrall.

'Rummaging through the wilderness after a ghost, being propositioned by colleagues, making babies, and now the new company CEO. I should think that they all qualify as busy.'

'You knew!' A feeling of betrayal swept through him. 'So, who's been giving you all the grubby details?'

'Never mind that right now.' She reached forward, gently grasping his arm, turning him towards that exit. 'Let's get out of here, get home to wherever you're living now, so we can talk.'

'What?' he said. 'You don't know where I live?'

'Now, don't get narky,' she said, laughing. 'I'll reveal everything after I've washed off this travel dust, we've been to bed, and I've got a glass of fine wine in my hands.'

The lure of bed and quiet conversation stilled Harry's questions as they bustled to the exit through the milling crowd, to the car sequestered in the multi-storeyed, monolithic, concrete car park – hostile traffic, the occasional rain shower, conversation sparse with the threat of truth. This moment bellowed opportunity, possibility, though Harry wasn't sure what that meant for his future.

*

Anika looked at Harry from the lounge, the rim of the glass between her lips. A penetrating look gave way to quizzical, then, as if a decision had been reached, she said, 'Nice wine. So, they're not certain yet?'

'Pretty much there with their prognosis, though these people work with statistics, variances, probabilities and so on. Thirty per cent is a good chance for them.' Harry couldn't disguise the sadness in his voice.

Harry still felt the heat of their union, the softness of the bed, her body, wanting the feeling to last, to push away the distressing things in his hitherto unruly life. Yet, here was Anika, focusing on what needed to be addressed, refusing to slide away from reality, from what ultimately might intrude on their relationship.

'But there is a chance, I mean, a chance she could pull through?' Anika wanted to get to the nub, the answer.

'Chance? Low, very low,' he said. 'But, yes, a chance.'

'So, Sophie needs looking after,' Anika said, finality in her voice. 'At least until Frances is free of all this ...' Harry could see even Anika wanted to dodge that word. '... this cancer.'

'Anika, the odds are against any recovery. The child, Sophie,' he said, shaking his head, 'may be my responsibility forever.' He had to start relating to Sophie at a more personal level.

Anika lowered the glass. 'Yes, I know the odds are poor, Harry, but we've got to stay positive,' she said, 'for both of them.'

The use of *we* made Harry pause. Did Anika mean to embroil herself in this mess?

'Harry, I've seen people recover from the most hopeless situations, places where they've been driven to abandon everything, to the point of suicide. Bangladesh, even my god-forsaken family. And yet, they recovered and eventually even prospered. Why? Because they didn't lose hope.'

'You don't need to stick with this, Anika. You've given enough of yourself to others.'

'It's not a case of giving!' Harry could see the passion as Anika placed her wine glass to the side, brimming with a thirst for something he couldn't quite understand. 'It's respect, respect for the lives of others, for their right to exist, right to prosperity, and a chance for the wonderful things this earth can offer, for ...' She stopped, a sudden smile breaking across her face. 'Can't help preaching, can I?'

Harry sober. 'I'm saying you're free to leave if you want to. That's all.'

Anika paused as if considering the offer, the smile growing. 'Not yet, Harry, not until you tell me to go.'

Anika leaned forward and said, 'Do you want me to go?' her smile slowly fading.

This was the crux of his dilemma, the paradox he had wrestled with since his first sight of Anika. Selfish, but she was the wellspring of his redemption, the catalyst for release from the chains of the past. Yet, was it callous vanity to place such a burden on another?

'I want you to stay more than you could ever know,' he said.

'I know,' she said, drinking the last of the wine and offering the empty glass to Harry. 'I think I need a refill.'

*

Harry rang Jessica and told her about his recent surrender to obligation or duty, or whatever it might be called. Her response was predictable.

'I reckon. I've found another lead for Jimmy,' she said.

Harry took a breath. 'Did you hear me, Jessica? There are things I've got to do here, people depending on my actions, my commitment.'

'It's a good one.' Jessica was undeterred by Harry's newfound concerns. 'Wallaga Lake. I reckon that's where he ended up.'

Realising that resistance was pointless, Harry submitted to Jessica's excitement. 'Where?'

'Wallaga Lake.' A patient tone in Jessica's voice, the repetition penetrating his mental fog.

'Yes.' Harry remembered. *Too much rattling around in my mind*, he thought. 'Near Bermagui, on the coast?'

'Yeah, near where we found the diary.' He could hear the elation in her voice. 'I'm headed there on the weekend. You coming?'

'Jessica, I'm rather tied up with things here. You know, responsibilities?'

'That's a new one for you, Harry. I mean, being responsible for something, or rather, wanting to be responsible.'

'Yeah, well, I guess it comes to us all.' He wanted to shut this conversation down – why he had called Jessica at all confounded him. 'I just can't spare the time now, traipsing around looking for ghosts.'

'This responsibility lark has really got you by the balls, hasn't it?'

Harry could hear the goading tone in Jessica's voice. He couldn't prevent a caustic response. 'I have no choice, Jessica. People are depending on me.'

A moment of silence on the line.

'Harry, if you really can't get away from your *responsibilities* ...' Harry flinched at the emphasis, 'then I guess I'll lumber on by myself, keep chipping away at the evidence. But ...' A deep breath echoed through the phone, '... this is a really good chance, and you being there would mean everything. We've been in this together from the beginning.'

'Your brother, what about him? Couldn't he lend a hand?'

A strained laugh. 'You reckon you've been irresponsible. That silly bugger has reinvented the meaning of the word. He's totally unreliable!'

'Still,' Harry said forcefully. 'He's family. And he can help with the digging, the ferreting through all the lost history.'

Jessica laughed again, the strain now mirthless. 'I haven't a clue where he is. He's gone to ground somewhere, hiding from those Sydney crooks, the ones he took the money from and didn't deliver the goods.' A pause. Harry imagined the shaking head as if she was repelling an annoying insect.

'They wouldn't know he was down there.' Harry didn't want to let the opportunity fade.

'Oh, yes! They did. Turned up in town, looking for him. That's when he scarpered. Took off like a frightened rabbit.'

Harry didn't know what to say – he had no further digressions.

'No uncles, aunts or cousins to join in the hunt?' he said, trying to suppress the desperation in his voice.

'No.'

'No? Jessica, you've got relatives everywhere!'

'Yeah, I'm talking to one right now. Cuz.'

Harry took a breath. Of course, she was right. Whether he liked it or not, whether it was convenient or not, there was an obligation, a commitment to his broader family, to someone who needed his help, to Jessica.

Capitulation was the only strategy now. Harry knew when he was beaten, when to surrender, and when to make the best of a bad situation.

'Right. Well, when were you thinking of going to Wallaga Lake? he said, hoping the opportunity would be deferred to the distant future.

'This weekend. I've rung the people at the settlement, and they're okay with us being there.'

'A bit presumptuous, wasn't it? I mean, organising it when you didn't know whether I'd be there.'

'I knew,' she said. 'I knew you'd come.'

That about sums it up, Harry thought. *Understood better by everyone, manipulated by all and sundry, and protected from himself by those who thought they knew better – Ruth, Frances, Anika, Andy, and now Jessica.*

'Nice to be needed,' he said, almost to himself.

'Wouldn't go that far, Harry.'

'What?'

'Wanted maybe,' she said emphatically.

'What do you mean?' Harry didn't have an adequate response.

More laughter, this time Jessica's short, mischievous chuckle. 'Well, you know, men,' Jessica said. 'Useful for their brawn. Me man, lift heavy things, that sort of stuff.'

Harry felt the prick of irritation. This increasingly deprecating conversation needed to end.

'Well, as useless as you might consider me,' said Harry,' it's nice to be wanted for something.'

Jessica laughed. 'See you at the weekend then. I said we'd be there early Saturday morning.'

'Locked in, then.' There was resentment in his voice. 'The beach house. Friday night. You bring the booze. Dinner's on us.'

A pause. Silence on the line. 'Us?' said Jessica. Suspicion?

'Yeah. Me, Sophie and Anika.' Harry's turn to be presumptuous, their attendance far from guaranteed.

'Ah, yes. Your newfound responsibilities. Looking forward to meeting Sophie and Anika and the new you.' A sharp click as the phone line cut.

Harry tossed the phone onto the seat beside him. How could he deal with Jessica's problems as well as his mounting pile of issues? *Weak as usual,* he thought, *easier to acquiesce than to refuse, to accept the demands of others, sliding away from confrontation and anything like commitment or controversy, to the easy solution. They wanted him and sought him out to do their bidding. Shit! Was it arrogance that made him involve Anika in the pursuit of ghosts and the care of a child that was not hers?*

'So, where are we going?' Anika said as she emerged from the bathroom, vigorously rubbing a towel through her damp hair.

'Couldn't help hearing bits of that conversation.'

'The beach house,' he said, hastily adding, 'if you're okay to come?'

Anika stood silent for a moment, and Harry thought she was maybe pondering the prospect of slumming it in rural rustic charm. Finally, she said, 'I love that place. The forest, the beach, everything. When do we go?'

'I've got to clear it with Frances first. See if it's okay to take Sophie.'

'Yes, you aren't footloose anymore.' Harry wondered if the loss of freedom would see the last of Anika – freedom was a precious thing, a prize worth keeping, worth fighting for.

'Frances will probably want Sophie with her.' Was that likely amidst the rigours of chemotherapy and the resultant debilities?

'Maybe, but I've seen friends go through all that. It takes all the time between sessions to recover, and the concerns of others aren't on the priority list.' Anika paused, memory in her eyes. 'She may be glad of your ministrations.'

Ministrations? A strange way to describe the duty Harry felt, something he owed, a need that applied as much to himself as anyone else.

'I'll call her. See if it's alright,' he said, turning to the balcony and the privacy he felt was needed for such a call.

CHAPTER 19

THREATS

September 9

They drove south to the beach house, with "everything including the kitchen sink", as his father used to say of the hordes of vacationers that cluttered the roads every Christmas. Harry was used to simple travel – himself, the clothes he wore, maybe a toothbrush and shaving kit, nothing more. How could someone so small demand such an extensive wardrobe? Anika was as economical as Harry, but Sophie's stuff filled the car. Maybe even the kitchen sink was in there; Harry had lost count.

The first evening, Jessica laid out her plan – first the Aboriginal Land Council in Eden, seeking any available information: the lives of the displaced, the disinherited, the people forcibly removed from their ancestral lands to foreign jurisdictions, then to Wallaga Lake, the last resting place of so many of those with elusive origins.

Harry subsided into the magic of the beach house, calm, cosy, and peaceful. *It might take a bomb to shift me*, he thought, as the sunshine filtered through the banksia forest onto the broad deck. He closed his eyes, savouring the warmth and the distant crash of the surf, and felt himself drifting away, visions of Anika, their love-making carrying him to where he wanted to dwell, the strains of Sanibel floating from the stereo. They could make their whole life here, the rest of them – the ambitious crowd, the rapacious, grasping crowd, the world – held at bay. Harry tumbled into the dream.

'Harry.'

He resisted the pull.

'Harry!'

Eyes open. 'Yes, it's a beautiful day.'

Anika stood before him, forever calm, eternally alluring. 'Too nice to miss,' she said. 'Jessica's here, though, and she's ready to head to the Land Council.'

Harry drew a deep breath, nodded, walked to the stairs, down to the waiting car, and south to the Eden metropolis.

All the way, Jessica burbled on about the prospects for the final resolution of the Jimmy mystery, the chance they had to identify at last his final whereabouts. 'It has to be down here, Twofold Bay, Boydtown or Wallaga Lake,' she said more than once.

They separated after reaching the town, Anika and Jessica seeking the local Aboriginal Land Council representatives. Jessica was leaving no stone unturned, and Anika was curious about their search. Harry decided to check out the wharf; he remembered all those years ago as a youth, drinking beer to oblivion at the end of the wharf, then somehow driving home to be deposited, almost comatose, on his parents' doorstep by charitable friends.

Nostalgia! He didn't know whether it was better to leave it behind or be amazed at survival amid such stupidity.

The wharf was a stark outline against the glittering bay, with yachts and fishing vessels crowding against the stone walls. Harry strolled towards the far point of the dock, stood for a moment at the end, amongst memories, and turned, almost colliding with a short, squat, broken-faced man.

Harry recoiled. He didn't like the look of the character.

The man smiled, more a grimace, showing uneven teeth. His boss wanted to talk to him, he said, reaching out a hand to shepherd him towards the head of the wharf.

Harry wasn't sure. Submission seemed such a gutless response.

They walked casually up the hill towards the main town centre to a waiting black car.

'Strange place, this,' the Boss said, holding a large beaker full of a nondescript liquid as he stood before Harry in the dimly-lit hotel room.

Harry wondered what was strange.

'I mean, what do people do here, apart from walking the dog?'

Was a comment required? 'There was a fishing industry,' Harry said, 'and a cannery.'

'Yeah, I know, but that went years ago, didn't it?'

'Yes, they overfished the tuna and basically killed their industry.'

'So, now they just walk the dog?'

Harry had no response. This conversation must have some purpose, though he couldn't see it just yet.

The Boss took a small sip from the glass tumbler, pursing his lips as he savoured the taste, leaning against the small table extending from a kitchenette.

Silence.

'It's like this, Harry. It is Harry, isn't it?'

Harry nodded, wondering how this thug knew his name and where to find him, why he had agreed to come to this place, and why he had submitted once again to the demands of others. Convincing Frances to allow Sophie to join him had been relatively easy. However, he saw her regret, despite the sense of devolving responsibilities while she underwent treatment and the sadness that separation would bring. Anika surprised Harry; she matched her words with enthusiasm, embracing the opportunity to spend time with Sophie. Was this a selfish surrogacy, an attempt to purloin the affection of another person's child?

'We're looking for Jim. You know Jim?'

Harry drew a deep breath. Should he brazen it out with denial or make a full confession? He decided on a middle path.

'Yes, I know *a* Jim, who doesn't,' said Harry. 'Possibly not the one you're looking for, though.'

'No, we're looking for a specific Jim, Harry. Jim from Bombala. The specific Jim that came to this god-forsaken place several weeks ago, with you, I believe, down the mountains through the bush. We reckon you know his whereabouts.' A smug arrogance seeped from the words.

Harry thought for a moment. So that was it – Jim, the lurk merchant, the dabbler in dark quarters, the would-be dealer in illicit substances. Was denial really an option? And how the hell did they know so much about his movements? He glanced across at the goon standing quietly by the door to the hotel room, at the thighs like tree trunks, biceps straining at the shirt sleeves, the slight bulge near the left armpit.

Harry nodded, shuffling his feet. He *could* make a break for it through the window. He might be all right – it wasn't too far to the ground from this first floor, but where would he go, supposing he wasn't injured in the fall? To the police, with Jim's notable illegal activities and his life hanging by a thread? Disappear like Jim? Live in anticipation of another visit, at an inopportune moment, from a less convivial felon?

A sudden image of Anika and Sofie!

Harry felt his heart jump, an electric shock almost buckling his legs.

Had Anika been approached by these thugs?

Where were they now? He guessed they were still in town?

He focused on the man leaning casually before him against the small table.

'I haven't seen the Jim I know for weeks. He led me through the pass from the high country. We parted company when we arrived here, and I didn't question him about his business dealings. Don't know where he is now?' Harry hoped his voice didn't show any of his anxiety.

The Boss raised a questioning eyebrow.

'You know, Harry, I find that hard to believe.'

Harry shrugged. *Time to go on the offensive,* he thought. Compliance and cooperation with these thugs were getting nowhere. 'I'm afraid I can't help you, Mister ...?' Harry craned his neck forward enquiringly. 'What did you say your name was?'

'Didn't,' the Boss said, face suddenly expressionless. 'He owes us. We paid him, he didn't deliver the goods. Simple as that. So, we'd like to talk with him so's we can clear the matter up.'

Harry was sure it would be more than *just a talk*.

Time to go.

'Well, it been nice talking to you, Mr ...? Whatever your name is. I've got things to do, people to meet. So, if there's nothing else, good luck with your search for Jim. I'm sure he'll turn up if you hang around here long enough.' Harry backed towards the door, eyes firmly fixed on the Boss, expecting collision with the obdurate form of the door goon.

The Boss' eyes flicked up, and he gave a slight nod, face impassive.

Harry heard the click of the door latch. *This is where things get really unpleasant*, he thought. He tensed, expecting a fist in the back or at least the restraining weight of a burly arm.

A slight air draft brushed Harry's neck as he turned towards the door. *Here it comes*, he thought. *That enormous fist will slam into my face, and I'll go down like a sack of potatoes.*

He turned.

An open door, a stairway down to the street beyond, a clear path to freedom, and the sense that any getaway would inevitably be prevented. Harry moved forward anyway, confidence in his step that he didn't feel.

The top of the stairs was a milestone, Harry unsteady at the drop to liberty, a receding voice saying, 'See you again, Harry. And tell Jim when you see him, we'll be right behind.'

Harry said nothing, looking only forward, careful to appear

calm and unhurried as he descended to the street. He silently cursed Jim. This was a world in which he had no part; Jim had no right to bring Anika, Sofie, or even Jessica into the orbit of these hoodlums.

Harry squinted as he walked through the hotel doorway, onto the street, into the bright sunlight. He scanned left then right, hoping to glimpse Anika or Jessica outside the few shops along the main road. Groups of shoppers loitered along the footpath about the craft-shop window displays.

Harry took a deep breath, dread rising; no familiar faces, no idea where to turn, no time to waste. They needed to quit this place. He dug into his pocket, retrieved his buried phone, and dialled Jessica, the dial tone broadcasting the urgency he now felt.

A click!

'Yes?' Jessica's voice.

'Are you with Anika?'

'Nice to hear from you, Harry.' *Jessica's treating my call as a joke,* Harry thought.

'Are you with Anika and Sophie?' A firm voice, more emphasis this time.

'No.' A pause. 'What's the problem, Harry?'

'Where are they?' And, where are you?'

'They've gone for a walk to the wharf,' Jessica said, voice registering a new concern. 'And I'm at the Land Council office, just finishing up here.'

'Great,' from Harry, though hardly feeling the greatness. 'Get to the car. Pick us up at the wharf.'

'Harry, what's going on?'

'I'll tell you when you pick us up.' Harry took a breath, preserving calm in his voice. 'But it's about that brother of yours and the goons who are after him. We've got to get out of town and fast.'

'I won't be long,' said Jessica. 'Just a few more minutes here to finish up.'

'No, Jessica.' Harry felt anger mixed with panic rising. 'Now! You need to come now!'

Silence on the line.

'Now!' said Harry, not caring that he now showed the alarm he felt.

*

Harry was silent, looking away, watching the mix of forest and farms float by as they drove north, along the back road to the beach house, Jessica at the wheel – on the run! Was this how their lives would be now, their safety, security, and well-being compromised by the casual folly of one person?

The rush to the wharf was desperate. Harry ran the whole way, searching for Anika and Sofie, hoping to see them before they reached the harbour or decided to wander elsewhere. The bright sunny day with a gentle cool breeze from the south belied the dark cloud he saw in his mind – the storm engendered by the criminal ambitions of the Boss, his cronies and Jim. The moment Harry rounded the last corner onto the boat-lined wharf, he saw Anika as she bent forward, peering intently at a small fishing boat resting below the dockside, talking animatedly to a curious Sofie balanced on her hip. He stopped, almost beguiled by the calm of the place, people casually basking in the sunshine about the wharf, the backdrop of metal lines clinking against masts, Anika and Sofie quietly enthralled by the nautical spectacle. Where was the urgency here? Surely no threat could penetrate this idyll?

A sudden screech!

Harry looked behind, expecting to see that same black vehicle as it slid into one of the parking bays at the head of the wharf.

Nothing. The road was clear.

Again, a screech! This time above.

Harry looked skyward.

Gulls. Big gulls wheeling in anticipation of the odd chip or crumbs from the tourist's leavings.

With a deep breath and a slight shake of his shoulders, his attention once again on the two figures along the wharf, Harry strode purposefully towards Anika. She seemed to sense his presence, turning towards him as he approached, a broad smile flashing across her face, framed by the cascade of thick straight hair. She whispered a word in Sophie's ear as both now focused on Harry's approach.

'We need to leave,' he said softly, reaching out to gently touch Anika's arm – he didn't want to create alarm.

'It's a sunny day, Harry,' Anika said, still smiling. 'And the boats are fascinating.'

Harry immediately voiced his fears. 'Has anyone suspicious approached you, asking questions?

'No!' Anika said, shaking her head, the smile dropping from her face.

'I've just been menaced by a bunch of heavies. They're looking for Jim, Jessica's brother. You know, the one I walked with to the coast from Bombala.'

'Why? Do they reckon you know where he is?'

'I think they were probing, trying to find out who might know where he is.'

'Do you?'

'No, Jessica might have some clues, but she's not saying.'

Anika stood silent, frowning, thoughts playing across her face, contrasting to the wharf's gentle sunshine and cheerful, benign activity.

'So, we need to get out of here before they force you, Sophie, and Jessica into being a focus for their search,' Harry said without waiting for further questions.

'Jessica!' said Anika. 'Did you warn her?'

'Yes, she's on her way with the car.'

Anika raised her free hand and pointed. 'I think she's arrived.'

Harry turned and saw their vehicle swinging into the car park; they hurried to their salvation.

*

'He asked questions, simple, but ones containing a comment as well. You know, like a lawyer would if they had you in the dock,' Harry said. They sat on the beach house deck, Anika and Jessica watching, silently scrutinising him, searching, he guessed, for signs of the panic that he knew was waiting to shatter his veneer of calm.

'You've got experience with the dock, have you, Harry?' Anika had found her voice.

Jessica drew a breath, mouth open as if to say something, remaining quiet as she slumped back on the settee, eyes focused on the distance.

'Is there something we need to know, Jessica?' said Harry.

Jessica's eyes flicked to Harry.

Silence, except for the light breeze brushing through the banksia forest about the beach house, the distant crash of the surf a backdrop.

'No, better you don't know.'

'How's that,' said Harry. 'If it's about Jim, then better we know.'

The faint beat of the waves.

'If these bastards turn up and threaten you, then better you don't know.'

'As I said, how's that work, Jessica? If these bastards turn up, knowledge like that will likely be our get-out-of-trouble card!' Harry was fed up with prevarication.

Mouth tight, Jessica stood, wandering slowly into the kitchen; the clatter of cups, the hiss of the jug set to boil. 'Anyone for a cuppa,' she said. *A cheerless voice*, Harry thought, reflecting his resignation and their hostile situation.

The universal panacea: a cup of tea!

Harry looked across to Anika, one eyebrow raised, a slight tilt to her head; the message: *Back off, let me deal with this*. Anika rose from the comfort of the old couch at the end of the deck, following Jessica. Harry sat, remembering the fear at interrogation, the veiled threat of reprisal with non-cooperation, examining possible way-forward alternatives:

Sacrifice Jim to the mob.

Sacrifice Jim to the police.

Hide – head for the hills and hope that anonymity could be preserved.

Not a good set of options, he thought. *Low chance of success.* He laughed, the first for some time.

'What's funny?' said Anika. Harry looked up, dragging himself from his thoughts. Anika stood before him, calm as always, with a quizzical expression.

'Just thinking through our go-forward options,' he said. 'None of them are enticing.'

'Well, here's something to think about,' Anika said as she sat on the old couch. 'Jessica's not sure, but she believes Jim's headed north and west, up to Kamilaroi country, around Walgett, maybe Coonabarabran.'

'Why the bloody hell would he go there? Fewer people there, they could ferret him out easily.'

'Yes, but lots of cousins, and you can see someone coming for miles.'

Harry nodded. 'So, do we leave him to his own devices, or do we find him and warn him about these goons.'

'Jessica reckons we just leave him alone for the time being. If we go traipsing out there, we might lead these bad guys right to him.'

Harry nodded again. He just wanted freedom from the mess of others – he had enough of his own chaos to manage, but leaving Jessica alone with her brother's turmoil and the danger it brought, didn't sit well.

'Right,' Harry said, not wishing to go further with the matter, 'but Jessica might be in the line of fire from these goons.'

Anika frowned, a slight creasing of her forehead that heightened her appeal. 'Jessica realises that. Reckons she can dodge the bullets.'

Harry laughed despite the gravity of the situation. 'She's a bullet-dodger now, is she?'

'No.' Jessica walked from the kitchen, balancing three cups of steaming tea. 'Here, brought you a cup even though you didn't say yes or no.'

'Nothing like a good cup of tea, I always say.' Harry was overdoing the part, exaggerating the sarcasm. 'No, what?' he said as he accepted the cup.

'I mean no, there'll be no bullets, no, I won't have to dodge them, and no, these crims won't bother us here or anywhere.'

This can't have a simple solution, thought Harry, *an ending that will mean these crims just go away.*

'That can't be right,' said Harry. 'They've already established the connection between Jim and me and located us down here. God knows what they know and who else they've connected with us.'

Jessica nodded, smiled and said, 'No, if I can negotiate a payment plan with them.'

Harry laughed; a cynical, staccato laugh that made the two women flinch. 'And just how in the hell are you going to achieve that, not the least find the cash flow to make it worth their while?'

Silence for a moment. Jessica rolled her tongue across her top lip, teeth taking hold of the bottom. 'Just yet, I don't know,' she said.

'That scaly brother of yours can't be relied on to do diddly squat,' said Harry. 'He's just hightailed it to the back blocks where he reckons he might be safe.'

Jessica said. 'It's worth a try.' She paused, Harry supposing she was sifting through possible solutions. Finally, she looked at Harry, a hard stare amidst the silence, saying, 'There is one other way we could expunge the debt.'

'Oh, yes. What's that?' Harry couldn't think of one that didn't involve the sacrifice of Jim.

'You stump up the money.'

'You're joking!' Harry said, almost a shout, his eyes flicking between the two women. 'Why would I spend money to appease these bastards with no realistic way of recovering the money?'

Jessica smiled a predatory grin. 'Because Harry, it's in your best interest. Think of it as an investment in the future, your future and the future of your family. If these guys are settled, they won't keep being a menace that might blow up when you least expect it.'

Harry was silent for a moment as he weighed the sense of such a plan and the uncertainty surrounding their predicament.

'No!' Harry said finally – he felt the reality of his own life in what he was about to say. 'That brother of yours needs to front up to his mistakes.' He looked across at Anika, feeling her warmth, the truth in his words, and his fumbling progress towards redemption.

Harry watched the play of emotion flash across Jessica's face: a scowl, cold and forbidding at first, replaced by resignation. 'I guess option one, then,' she said at last. 'I negotiate.'

'Jessica,' Harry jumped in. 'You do have another option.'

'Oh yes, what?'

'The police. You get your brother to admit to what he was part of. The coppers can then go after the bloody crims and perhaps shut them down. That way, Jim has a chance at deliverance, and the crims are off our backs.'

Jessica opened her mouth, Harry imagined in protest, then closed it. He could see her indecision, her face registering the conflict; so much to consider, so much at stake – family, reputation, possible conviction if Jim didn't frame the confession properly, the betrayal that such a strategy might mean.

The moment ticked away in silence. Harry looked again at Anika; with a wan half-smile, she held his eyes, a soft, caring, supporting gaze – he knew then that his approach was correct, perhaps the only viable option.

'I'll talk it through with Jim,' said Jessica. There was no bitterness or recrimination in her voice, just resignation. 'But before I do, we must visit the cemetery at the Wallaga Lake settlement. The Land council reckon we might find something there about my grandfather, Jimmy. Jessica was back on song.

Chapter 20

Confrontation

September 10

In the night, quiet, except for the gentle evening breeze from the sea through the trees, Harry dreamed, images mixed with emotion, the jumbled vision of the high mountains, the hidden pass to the coast, the cave of veiled wonders, a man walking boldly, leading a magnificent horse across a ruined landscape. Harry went too far, desperately backing away from the emaciated inhabitants of a village, a wreck surrounded by thick jungle, swamp that clawed at the margins, bringing the cloying smell of decay and inevitability. If only he could demonstrate the guts necessary to move forward, to save the ones he loved. Anika was there, Sophie too, and maybe even Jessica, though she would probably argue that she was not. He looked skyward through the bending branches, at the thick, tropical leaves, feeling suddenly awkward so close to the ground, realising he was only able to move by digging fingers into the moist, humus-laden soil, dragging his body forward across the leaf-littered ground, moving painfully slowly towards the group of hollow-eyed villagers, a group of poor souls that recoiled in dread, horrified at what approached them. Harry knew now he wouldn't make it, that

Anika and Sophie were beyond his reach, beyond the capacity of his broken body.

He woke, still saturated by the sensations, wanting to return to complete his task, rose from the bed, and stumbled through the house to the deck where the cool night air seemed to brush away his distress, fatigue, and fears.

When the dark eventually slackened, hinting at a change in the east, the moment of false dawn, Harry quietly padded back to bed into the arms of a drowsy Anika, her smooth skin, her warmth dispelling the last of his dreams. He slept deeply, dreamless, until a car door slam jerked him half awake, a key in the front door bringing him into the new day.

Jessica trundled up the stairs, the clatter of her boots on the timber steps a sort of military tattoo, Harry thought, a call to arms against a world that threatened to deny her the resolution she needed, a declaration that she was here, still cutting a swathe through the opposition of others.

Harry stood at the kitchen bench fiddling with the coffee machine, his daily ritual, his homage to morning cappuccinos. 'Like a coffee, Jessica?' he said, as she reached the top step.

Jessica looked startled for a second. 'Gee, Harry, you're up early.'

'Couldn't sleep,' he said.

'It's the sun,' she said, smiling. 'Bloody thing keeps getting up earlier every day. Sparrow fart for me every day.'

Harry pushed a full cup across the bench. 'So, here's a coffee to keep you awake, or sane, or whatever, guaranteed not to put you to sleep.'

Jessica accepted the cup, Harry decanting another brew into an oversized mug. She dropped onto the old couch, taking a long swig of the coffee. 'Not bad,' she said, brushing away the foam remnants about her top lip. 'Maybe you should get a job as a barista.'

'Don't think my budget could stand the pay cut,' Harry said.

'Come on,' Jessica said, laughing. 'Change is as good as a holiday, and after yesterday, I reckon you need one.'

'Too many responsibilities.' Harry was feeling contrary, despite Jessica's sound logic; he didn't cope well with lack of sleep or a cheerful audience so early in the morning. 'So, what are your plans today, Jessica.'

Jessica sat quietly for a moment, her eyes making a curious circle to the ceiling and then back to Harry, *An outward manifestation,* Harry thought, *of the wheels turning, her mind churning through options and possibilities, making a list – Jessica always had a To Do list.*

'Contact your brother.' The words came from the end of the room. Eyes pivoted to Anika as she emerged from the bedroom to sit on the dilapidated chair near the doors to the deck. 'That's got to be a priority, Jessica.'

'Yeah, well, easier said than done.'

'Why?' said Harry, with a spark of irritation. 'As soon as you can, you need to spell out the facts, tell him his options, get him into a cop shop to explain what's going on.'

'As I said, easier said than done. First, he needs to answer his phone. I tried that last night, but no luck. Second, without me standing in front of him, or rather standing *over* him, he's likely to just do another runner.'

Harry raised his hands, palms skyward, a surrender. 'Well then, another road trip, this time to wherever you reckon the scaly prick is.'

'Third, I'm not exactly sure where he is.'

'Bloody hell, Jessica,' Harry's frustration threatened to boil over. 'Call in the information you need from that vast family of yours. He's got to have contacted someone in his hurry to get away.'

'Yeah, doing that. But word hasn't come back yet.'

'Well then, ring them again and again until you get an answer.' Frustration finally boiled over into anger – how could he accept this lingering threat?

'It'll take a bit of time, Harry.' Anika said, pouring cool water over Harry's ire. 'In the meantime, we can stay here, enjoy the beach with Sophie, and spend some time in this beautiful place.'

Harry nodded. He was consumed by anger at the threat, this time a malfunction, not his own but that of another. But was anger the solution to anything? Anger could turn to hatred, spiralling to madness, hurting only one person – himself. He constantly blamed someone else for the predicament rather than accepting the situation, calmly acknowledging the good things in his life. She was right; he needed to call it a day to dispel the influence of this madness.

'Right,' he said with a sigh. 'You're right. I need to change my thinking, accept that we'll eventually get hold of Jim, hopefully convincing him that confession is best for us all.' Harry felt the tension release with that statement. He looked across to a smiling Anika, at a chortling Sophie toddling across the floor to climb onto the chair next to Anika, to Jessica pensively sipping coffee. Still, he couldn't help wondering where all this would lead. Were they just sticking their heads in the sand? Was the threat just a product of their overactive imagination? Could they survive the intrigues of those with criminal intent? Was this the haven they so desperately wanted it to be? Harry sighed again, walking towards the open deck, to the bird song from the coastal forest, the call of his beloved ocean, towards the freedom he so wanted.

'I've arranged a meeting with the people at Wallaga Lake,' said Jessica from the silence. 'So, we can take a look at the cemetery. It's on the point next to the lake. Tomorrow morning.'

Harry rested his elbows on the deck balustrade, gazing absently into the trees. Jessica was relentless, forever focused on the next objective. When would he be free of her zeal? As he pushed himself to respond, heaving himself upright and turning towards the room, his phone rang.

He dug the phone from his pocket and fumbled it to his ear.

'Harry?'

'Yes, Andy.'

'It's Teresa.'

'What? What about her?'

'She's hatched a coup, got some of the board members to support her. She's out for blood.'

'What the hell do you want me to do?'

'Well, you're the new CEO, and you should be here to help fight this off.'

Harry turned to the assembled women, a mixture of foreboding and relief. 'Can we delay the cemetery? There's a bit of a crisis at work in Sydney. I've got to head there now.'

*

September 11

This wouldn't do anyone any good, including the company's fortunes. Teresa was in a wrecking mood, fulfilling the objectives of a corporate psychopath, delivering chaos wherever she stepped. Part of the board members had fallen for her emotive diatribe, accusations that perhaps resonated with their own yearning for power: *Andy was two-faced, Harry weak and ineffectual, the company doomed unless the board dismissed them both without delay, returning the corporation to its core business, its professed strategy for growth. Teresa had a sure-fire plan to mobilise resources, marshal its people, and regain the shareholders' support.*

Bullshit, though, Harry had to admit, convincingly and passionately delivered.

Harry had no doubt that rejection played a big part in this destructive game, kicking himself that he hadn't seen it all coming: he was intimately aware of Teresa's desire for control, so why hadn't he quashed it before it took hold?

Lesson learned, he thought, *though perhaps a little late*. Andy stood gazing out the window at the sun-drenched harbour, Harry lounging on the couch that Andy had strategically positioned near the apartment balcony to catch the morning sun.

'Before we launch any counter-attack,' said Andy, 'we need to make sure she hasn't anticipated it and won't cut us off at the pass.'

'Listen, Andy, mate, I don't need or want any of this.' Harry just wanted to return to a stable life.

'Neither do I. But we can't let Teresa into the honey pot. They'll be nothing left if she succeeds, and everything we've worked to build will be gone in a flash.'

'So, sack her.'

'Not an option. It'd be in the courts before you could blink.'

'Maybe that's preferable to letting her run riot inside the company. Take the wind out of her sails.'

'And maybe you should marry her? Might defuse this ridiculous focus on destroying you and me with you.' Andy's counter-punch shut Harry up.

Silence for a moment. Harry persisted, 'Sacking her might be the only viable alternative. It would never reach court if we made an out-of-court settlement after a year or so. Legal fees, yes, but it would neutralise the immediate threat.'

'Geez, sacking people means so much complicated stuff, Harry. I prefer to move them sideways so they can make other plans and leave amicably.'

'Is that what you hoped I would do?' Harry said, laughing. 'You know Teresa will never leave amicably. She's the epitome of ambition and relentless to boot.'

'Yeah, you found that out in buckets!' Andy said, smiling, levelling his eyes at Harry. 'By the way, how's it going with Anika?'

'We'll have to work on the renegade board members as well. What's their beef?'

'Leave them to me.' Andy dismissed the concern with a sweep

of the hand. 'They're just stirring the pot, trying to figure ways they can benefit from a disturbance like this. I've already met them, and they're starting to waver.'

'Then, sack her. Get rid of her now. She's not essential to anything but her obsession with revenge.' Harry wanted this adventure closed, eager for stability in his life. His existence seemed to generate volatility; his life had become mere survival against a barrage of problems caused by others. He wondered whether he could sustain his new-found brutality.

'Harsh, Harry.' Andy startled. 'Never thought I'd see you embrace such a tactic.'

'Me neither,' Harry said with regret, 'but sometimes, it seems you have to be ruthless to keep things running properly.'

'You going to tell her?' Andy wanted to distance himself from the dirt.

'No, Andy, me approaching Teresa now would only reinforce her desire for revenge. And anyway, this sort of tactic is your forte.'

Andy winced, saying, with a sour note, 'Yes, the story of my life. I've become a pitiless bastard.'

Harry laughed. 'Better pitiless than trampled underfoot. And by the way, Anika and I are doing fine.'

CHAPTER 21

ENDINGS

September 15

Harry didn't read the media commentary. Nothing in any of the reporting could accurately explain what had happened or add anything to what he already knew or didn't want to know. He left unconsumed the last of his coffee, paid at the till, and walked the long stretch from the café through the city to the apartment, where he rang Andy – a more reliable source of intel than the rumour-mongering tabloids. Andy answered with a sharp sound in his voice, an animal bark, impatience that Harry could only guess resulted from difficult interviews with difficult people.

'So, it went well, did it?' Harry said. 'She rolled over and played dead.'

'What are you talking about?'

'Teresa. We move ahead now, free of all that angst.'

'Hardly. Have you seen the papers?' said Andy.

'No, I try to avoid fiction.'

'Teresa's managed to contact the lot, including the scandal sheets and magazines. I feel like a maligned celebrity, fallen and disgraced. They'll be tapping our phones next, delving into my love

233

life – if I had one.'

'So, what happened, Andy.'

'I not only got an earful, but she also threatened me with everything just short of death, claimed breach of promise from you, and vowed to destroy us both, in the media and in court.'

'Yeah, went well then.' Harry imagined the scene. 'Or at least as expected.'

'Expected? Yes, I suppose so, though not ended yet. She's out of the office at least, I've brought the errant board members to heel, or compliance. So, we can at least follow the plan we discussed – but mate, you need to be here, in the office, dealing with any fallout.'

Harry sighed. 'Yep, I'll head there now. Just as long as Teresa isn't loitering in some dark place, some dark corridor.'

'Look, Harry, Teresa's whole existence is some dark place, but now it's somewhere else, not here.'

'A face-to-face with her right now would be ugly, not to say totally non-productive.'

'Yeah, realise that. That's why I took the flak. But no more. From here on, it's all through the legals. They can deal with the angst. Let's get on with running this show.'

The trudge to the office was like a trek into the past – so long the absence of corporate bullshit, so long embroiled in Jessica's search, in the joy of Anika's presence. Andy met him at the entrance before he reached the lifts to the office: 'Television bloody crews,' he said. 'Turned up thirty minutes ago. Still setting up, so there's a chance we can dodge them.' He herded Harry to the subterranean carpark, saying, 'Change of plans. The city isn't safe now, so take my car and head for the beach house. We'll pick everything up next week. The media rabble should have calmed down by then.'

What could Harry say? Did Andy want him to object, to insist that staying was the thing to do? Could his presence right now, amidst this turmoil, solve anything, provide anything but a distraction? 'Ruth, my mother, and Frances need to be warned. The media mob will no doubt make those connections.'

'Leave that to me. I'll go see them both,' Andy said, as he opened the car door. 'Just fuck off for a while, but when you're back in the office in a week, it's full attention on what we need to do.'

Harry escaped the city bedlam and the demands of ex-lovers and the office. He drove south past the dark mass of Mt Dromedary, the remnant core of that ancient volcano, the shadowy monzonite crystals resisting extinction for almost one hundred million years, massing together as Gulaga, the mother, the source of spiritual identity; it emphasised the brevity of his existence, the triviality of aspirations, the insignificance of mistakes made in any one lifetime.

Though glad to be free from Sydney and the machinations of a ruthless crowd, even for a short time, the promise of more Jessica schemes instilled an edge to his beach house return.

*

September 20
Midmorning

'Turn here,' said Jessica.

'What, here, down the dirt track?' Harry said, as he carefully guided the car through the houses strung out along the road. The lump in the middle of the dirt track looked like it would scrape the bottom out of the vehicle.

'Yeah. It leads to Cemetery Point.'

'Hold onto your hat. This could be rough.' Harry swung the wheel sharply, angling the car over the crumbling verge onto the worn, rarely-used path.

'We can always walk,' Jessica said, amidst the clatter of the suspension as one side of the car climbed the earthen wall. The car tilted, Jessica desperately grasping at the door handle, Harry gripping the steering wheel as his shoulder crashed into the driver-side door. *Maybe their demise would be celebrated at the cemetery*, he thought. *Should have brought the old Landcruiser. No problem here with that old truck.*

'Not much used,' he said, shouting above the creaks and groans of the tortured suspension.

'The fella at the Land Council told me they'd done a lot of work down here.' Jessica defended her decision.

'Not on this road.' Harry was starting to worry about the structural integrity of the vehicle. First, their bush bash on Mt Dromedary, now this! Another bang, a crash, a groan; the track suddenly levelled, and they lurched past an overgrown brick wall into a clearing.

Harry killed the engine, flung open the door, and stood surveying a lightly grassed field, the glittering water of the lake just visible through a thick line of trees. He stood next to the car for a moment, bathed in the warmth of light dappled by the tall coastal eucalypts, lingering, mesmerised by the calm, the background bird noises, and the absence of calamity. *So different*, he thought, *to the electronic sterility of Frances' hospital room or the tense bareness of the Sydney office.* The memories seemed to consume him, vision turned inward.

'Come on, Harry.' Anika's voice.

The vision dissolved, focus returning to Jessica, closely followed by Anika leading Sophie as they walked down the hill towards the distant lake.

'The graves are this way.' Jessica shouting now from a distance.

Harry shivered, scattering the memory. He strode across the open ground, into the trees, to a cluster of renovated graves, each with a numbered silver tag placed on a crude ground-level plinth.

Jessica pulled a paper from her satchel, carefully examining the script. 'The numbered graves are the ones they've found, using ground-penetration radar,' she said. 'They can identify who's in most of them, but there's still lots without any record.'

'How far back?'

'Harry, aboriginal people have been here for thousands of years. There're middens all around the lake, including here. Up until the 1890s, the locals used this spot. It's sacred. But when the Aboriginal Protection Board was formed in 1883, the whole thing gradually fell apart. The locals lost their way, traditions were ignored in favour of the handouts and people from all over were shipped here. So, it wasn't just the local Yuin people anymore. Eventually, nobody could remember the traditions or how they all fitted together.'

'Jimmy? He was Kamilaroi from way out west of the ranges. Why do you reckon he came here?'

'Harry, I don't know if he was *here*, but we know he was close by at some point, up there on the mountain.'

'He's not listed there?' Harry pointed to the list in Jessica's hand.

'No. Could be one of the unknown ones.'

'Yeah. But we'll never know, Jessica.' Harry said, stating the bleeding obvious.

'I just thought I might get a feeling, you know, some sort of vibe if we came here, if Jimmy was here. Mum said Jimmy would let us know somehow.'

Harry could feel his scepticism leap into the believability void. Still, he held his tongue – maybe he was applying some sort of sensitivity at last?

'This list has a map with it,' said Jessica. 'It shows where the unknown graves are. Over here.' She pointed through the trees towards the water's edge. A downward slope, a transition onto rocky ground.

'Hard ground here, too hard to dig graves,' Harry said, as he followed Jessica. 'Let's face it, Jessica, it's a needle in a haystack.'

'I don't know, Harry, I can feel something,' Harry nodded. So, Anika was supporting Jessica now?

Jessica turned to face Harry, close to the water now, the cloudless sky a brilliant blue backdrop, the glistening water reflecting the midday sun. 'Yeah, I know, Harry, but I've got to try.'

Harry was silent, and he nodded. Anika wandered away beneath the trees, Sophie running forward to the water's edge.

Jessica raised her hand, pointing to a spot behind him. 'There's a grave, right there.'

Harry turned about, searching across the ground for a sign, anything that might represent a grave – all he could see was accumulated leaf litter, fallen branches, and the occasional rock sprouting from the ground.

'There!' Jessica said, elation in her voice.

Responding to Jessica's excitement, Anika turned from her examination of the shoreline.

Jessica quickly stepped forward, feet rustling through the accumulated ground debris from the sprawling eucalypts. She scattered a pile of dried leaves and branches with her boot revealing a series of small concentric circles traced on the ground with small, smooth speckled rocks. Harry stood mute: *How did she know that was there?* He approached the symbol, crouching to retrieve one of the stones, the heat from the midday sun radiating into his palm – *Monzonite, not from here,* he thought, *from the mountain, Gulaga, brought here from miles away.* He turned the stone slowly in his hand until the heat began to fade – a curiously comforting warmth that seemed to flow into his hand, along his arm, into his chest.

Anika arrived with Sophie, stooping to examine the artefact.

'This is a special place,' Jessica said, as she raised her eyes from the crude circles, searching their faces, her eyes sparkling with recognition.

'What?' he said, disbelief in his voice, though he knew what was coming.

'This is it,' she said.

'What? This is what?' Did he really need to ask?

'It's got to be.'

Harry rose from the stone circles. 'Now listen, Jessica. We've just found a pile of stones in a cemetery, which has been a burial ground for thousands of years.' Harry shook his head. 'It could be anyone.'

'It's him. This is where he is. Mum said I'd know, that Jimmy would tell me, tell us.'

'It's the place, the wind, imagination ...' Harry always sought a rational explanation.

A sharp noise, the crack of dry twigs, a sudden strengthening of the breeze.

Harry swung around, peering up the hill through the trees, expecting to see one of the local residents coming to tell them to leave this sacred place.

A silhouette flitted amongst the line of trees, more than a shadow.

For a moment, Harry questioned his sight, shifting his eyes to the sky – clear, no clouds.

A quick glance at Jessica and Anika – they stood, looking up the hill at the source of the spectre – transfixed.

'Did you see that?' Harry was looking for support and logic that could explain what he had seen.

'Yes.' Confirmation in unison from the two women – it was more than just his imagination, the consequence of an emotional breakdown.

'Yeah, I think I did. Maybe someone's horse has escaped?' Now it was Jessica's turn to favour reason over emotion.

Harry stood silent for a moment, peering into the vegetation, feeling uneasy. 'No,' he said at last. 'No, I've seen that horse before.' It was an acknowledgement of the fanciful.

'What do you mean, seen it before, Harry?' Jessica said, her voice turning shrill. 'We've never been here before.'

'Ah,' he said, feeling deflated. 'I saw that same horse in Israel when I stood on top of the walls of the Masada Fort.'

'Where?'

'The Masada Fort, it's an ancient mountaintop fortress in south-eastern Israel. The Jews had their last stand against the Romans there.'

'What the heck were you doing there?'

Harry didn't feel like explaining. 'Looking for evidence,' he said. 'Following my grandfather's footsteps in Palestine.' He had said enough to confirm any suspicion of his unsound mind.

'And the horse?'

'I saw it in the distance from the top of the fort.' He paused while he recalled that apparition. 'It looked just like this one.' It was an admission, a confession he had eschewed for too long.

Jessica stood quietly, teeth clamped against her bottom lip. Harry absorbed the moment, felt the quiet passage of time, the spell of the puzzle that had held them in thrall for so many weeks. 'Jimmy mentions a horse in the book,' she said at last.

'And there were the paintings of a horse in the cave.'

'Yes. Really, it was more than just a mention in the diary. More of an obsession. And remember,' Jessica said. 'Mum said the horse was more than just a horse to Jimmy.'

Harry remembered, hesitating. Acceptance of the vision seemed a betrayal, an abandonment of the rules, the precepts of his life, and his hold on reality.

'I've never told anyone about the horse at Masada,' Harry said, squinting up the hill, into the glare of the midday sun, searching for a recurrent vision. 'I always thought it was a figment of my overactive imagination, a silly emotional wish for something more, something more significant in this bloody hunt through the past.'

Anika shook her head. 'I saw it too, Harry. It's real. Or as real as something like that can be.'

Jessica quickly added: 'Mum never met Jimmy's horse, but she said Gurley, my grandmother, described him as the prince of horses, Jimmy's confidante, a confidante my grandmother could never access.'

Harry shook his head, 'Then why take him to Palestine, into such danger?'

'Because mum said they couldn't bear to be separated.'

Harry was struck dumb by the intensity of Jessica's words. He nodded, sighing as he scanned the hill for another sign. 'So, is this it then?' he said, breaking the silence. 'Have we found your illusive grandfather?' It sounded final. Was this an end to this all-consuming search?

Jessica turned, matching Harry's quiet attention to the hill. He could see her reluctance. Had she, both of them perhaps, grown so used to the search that leaving it would be impossible? He dwelt on the thought, *In adversity, opportunity, or was it, never let a chance go by?* The search had allowed him to understand his motivations and measure the impulses that had led him to nihilism and into the jurisdiction of those less interested in him than in their own welfare.

Perhaps the horse, even Jimmy, wanted an end to this odyssey: *Job done, quarry isolated, a message delivered by the universe.*

'I think we have, Harry.' Jessica slumped to the ground beside the stone circles amidst the dry, crackling leaves. 'Even if this isn't Jimmy, it doesn't really matter. It's irrelevant, really. What matters,' she said. 'Is understanding the past and how it's led us here. What matters is how we use what we've learned, how this can all mend the future.'

Harry exhaled, realising he had been holding his breath. He felt the release, for the first time in a while, contemplating a future, the prospect of a positive life: the cessation of a toxic relationship, the care of Frances, responsibility for an abandoned child, being with Anika, understanding of his own part in the continuum.

Harry thrust out his left hand to Jessica, embracing outstretched fingers, pulling her to her feet; he tightly held Anika's long fingers in his right. Silently, they walked side by side up the slope to the car parked at the cemetery entrance, a small child hopping beside them. The sun shone from a cloudless sky, the afternoon beckoned, and the future was fascinating.

*

"Hold my hand in yours, and we will
not fear what hands like ours can do."
The Epic of Gilgamesh

EPILOGUE

Since the last meeting, I have been wondering whether my opinions positively influenced the journey or merely served to confuse.

When the woman, Jessica, arrived so many months, maybe years, after our first conversation – for I have lost the ability to measure time – her path had taken a curious turn. Gone were the doubts she had held so close, absent also the desperate search for the cause of sufferings in generations past, replaced by a peaceful acceptance of her place in it all. She said the pathway to this harmony was knowledge of the outcome, a direct and personal connection with something other than understanding, past the realm of actual, beyond the reasonable.

If the future is unknowable, the past is at least partially discernible, not only through the actions of our forebears but perhaps also through our responses to the everyday. That knowledge, based on the immutable, the fixed, and the definite, must lend a surety to lives that otherwise would be lost. Jessica obviously thought so.

My discussion with her companion, Harry, laid bare the war that rages within so many of us: the conflict against ignorance, the battle between evasion and responsibility for oneself and others. Historians define greatness as victory over external forces, the subjugation of a tangible enemy – the greatest enemy, however, is the adversary within, the destructive impulse given form and substance within a frail mind, a foe that too often determines the fate of so many. Jessica showed me a journal, some might say the ramblings of a distressed mind, a memory they might say, so distorted that it could only be dismissed as erroneous, something remembered through a distorted prism. Harry started with that view, but I was inclined to view it as a vision without the lie inherent in interpretation. He left this isolated place satisfied with his version of events, though I believe he continues the journey, the voyage to some sort of understanding, looking for an accord with himself and those close to him.

Can we be sure of anything?

To maintain stability and our sense of self-worth, we must. Call it self-deception, if you will, but without the anchor of the past, a passion for the present and the promise of the future, everything becomes meaningless, the hollowness of existence crushing all purpose.

What happened on that day?

Jessica asserts that she rose from the ground – at the stones carefully arranged across the ground – to see Harry and Anika engrossed, their gaze fixed in the distance, up the hill. Her recollection of the order of events is unclear, but she saw movement, a shadow, a prominent figure moving amongst the trees at the brow of the hill. A voice, Harry's voice, she thought, alarmed and clearly distressed, exclaimed 'Horse!' Jessica maintained that it certainly could have been a horse, a magnificent beast, silver, shimmering as it emerged from the shadow of the trees.

Convincing?

Jessica was convinced. Harry had doubts; years of conditioning to scientific proof and logic were still a barrier to the miraculous, but despite his reservations and maybe because of the solid affirmation from Anika that the mirage was real, he found a peculiar peace in their situation. It was as if Jessica and Anika's interpretation of events absolved him of further travails, giving him licence to submit to the present, to an abandonment of the self-destructive, to the acceptance of love.

As I have said, I am unsure whether my listening and advice complicated matters or pushed anything towards resolution. I am sure, though, that there is more in heaven and earth than we will ever understand and that mankind will be forever trying to explain the mysterious, forever searching outward into the cosmos and delving inward, looking for a purpose to existence.

Whilst the future is impenetrable, the past is a book written solely for the benefit of the beholder. By its very nature, any retelling will be a distortion of fact. So, we rely upon the veracity of the storyteller, the exactness of the description, the interpretation, and trust in our ability to sift fact from falsehood, authenticity from bias, and validity from inaccuracy. I cannot claim my own telling of those stories is anything but distorted. Who could say that the outcome of those years and the responses of people caught in events beyond their control were predictable or fully explicable; certainly not me. Even the present is uncertain, its record manipulated by powers opaque to people. Only happenings close to us, within reach of our very eyes, can be relied upon as truth, unsullied by the interpretation of those determined to bend events to their purposes.

Dramatis Personae

Harry: Seeker of something he could never quite define, he continued as CEO of the company for another five years before abandoning the corporate world for the calm of his beach house. He accepted, without reservation, his responsibility for Sophie while immersing himself in his relationship with Anika, a bond that grew to define his very being. He became a writer of thoughtful fiction and an erstwhile landscape painter. He often said, 'If I can help just one person with my stories and messages of hope, I shall have achieved my aim.' He continued to challenge the surf on those big wave days, eschewing the crowds and cherishing the freedom of the ocean.

Frances: After a short schedule of radiotherapy, curtailed because of adverse effects, with repeated trials of chemotherapy, Frances succumbed to breast cancer. Harry was by her side when she died, vowing to never leave her alone, even to the last. She left all her possessions to Harry, which he duly maintained for Sophie, their daughter, when she came of age. Her ashes were buried, along with her mother, in a quiet, rural cemetery. The inscription above the grave states: *Brave beyond measure, conquered fear, celebrated life.*

Andy: Survival was the key to his life, reinvention in the corporate world, and rejuvenation through multiple marriages. Always loyal to his friendship with Harry, they frequently meet to discuss and laugh about the frenetic days surrounding Harry's identity crisis. He diversified his business interests until a stroke forced him to wind down his involvement in high-pressure commerce at the age of fifty-one. He now manipulates stocks and shares, independent of formal company trappings. He never again had any involvement with Teresa.

Teresa: The marshalling of resources, legal and publicity, against her onslaught quickly neutralised her as a direct threat, though there was always the suspicion that her relentless temper would somehow, sometime, bring her back into the fray – Teresa had lost the battle, but it was always feared, she would seek to win the war. She swiftly directed her attention to new targets, teaming up with a compliant partner, bearing one child, and promptly abandoning responsibility for her offspring to pursue global business interests. Her ascent to dominance as CEO, then chairman of the board of a medium to large company, was short-lived; however, her activities investigated when financial irregularities in the businesses she controlled were registered by the tax authorities. As a consequence, she was barred for life from holding office in any publicly listed company. To this day, Teresa lives alone, in obscurity.

Jessica: After witnessing the apparition at the Wallaga Lake cemetery, Jessica pursued a career in politics, rising eventually to a representative in the state parliament, through which she supported an indigenous voice in parliament, lending her persuasive voice to its adoption at both state and federal levels. Never again did she doubt the power of the past in all their lives whilst keeping level sight on what could be achieved in the present. Her campaigns usually extolled the slogan: *Listen to the past, embrace the future.* To this day, she maintains a gravitas appreciated and admired by all sides.

Ruth: Forever convinced of her dominion over family, Ruth continued to admonish Harry for his dereliction of Frances. Worried about Sophie's future at the hands of her wayward son, she continued to meddle, never acknowledging that time had passed and lessons had been learned, although new stability now pervaded the fortunes of her family. The past to Ruth had passed, better forgotten, never to be granted space in their lives and she continued in this vein until an apparition, termed a hallucination by many, including the medical experts – the ghost of her father, Sulli – exhorted her to journey to Palestine to meet with the descendants of his illicit liaison. To this day, she refuses to make the voyage, but her temper has been somewhat modified.

Jim: Surrendered to the police and was cautioned over his involvement in illicit drug deals; the Boss disappeared amongst the chaos that is Sydney, never brought to justice, and Harry and Anika never again faced the heavy hand of the criminal underworld.

Jimmy: His remains were never found. Despite his prominence, his magnetism, the drama that unfolded about his actions and his fortune, no evidence of his fate was ever uncovered. Along with

Horse, his faithful friend, he remains an enigma, a ghost with intriguing solidity, despite the passage of time, despite the myths and apologues that surround him. The best way to describe his being is a comparison with Gilgamesh, the Master of Animals, the survivor of the passage through hell and back again.